Bonnie Engstrom

Cindy's Perfect Dance

The Candy Cane Girls, book 2

By Bonnie Engstrom

Copyright © 2016 Bonnie Engstrom

Forget Me Not Romances, a division of Winged Publications.

All rights reserved as permitted under the U.S. Copyright Act of 1976. No part of the publication may be reproduced, distributed or transmitted in any form or by any means, or stored in a database or retrieval system, without prior permission of the publisher.

All verses from NIV version

This book is a work of fiction. Names, characters, places, and incidents are the product of the author's imagination and are used fictitiously. Any resemblance to actual events, locales, or persons, living or dead, is coincidental, except for the instances where they were used in conjunction with a business on purpose.

All rights reserved.

ISBN-13: 979-8-3302-5699-0

ACKNOWLEDGMENTS

First and foremost to my editor and publisher, Cynthia Hickey, at Forget Me Not Romances for patience while I lingered over this manuscript. This is the first one of my books that seemed to take forever to write.

To my psychologist husband, Dr. David Engstrom, Ph.D., who I interrupted from his online teaching and writing his own book a zillion times to ask questions about his expertise in Multiple Sclerosis.

To Marg Rodger, award winning florist and proprietor of North Scottsdale Floral, who kept thanking *me* for allowing her to help me choose flower selections for the bridal bouquet. She patiently pointed out blooms that would enhance it, then made a list and even gave me a stem of each. Those stems are in a pink vase on my kitchen counter for inspiration. I hope readers can visualize the beautiful bridal bouquet they helped to enrich, for it is truly outstanding.

To Kerrie Benvenuti and Carole Tompkins who helped with research finding me the perfect breakfast restaurant on Balboa Island. Long time Newport Beach friends are the best.

To Jill Stroope, wedding coordinator extraordinaire, who held my hand during the planning of three of my own children's weddings, and who held Kerstin Day's and Lydia Lovejoy's hands in both **Her Candy Cane Christmas** and **Her Valentine Promise**. Unfortunately, she is now retired. Maybe we Engstroms pushed her to her limit. I hope not.

To Miss Lorrie, preschool Bible teacher, who gave little Shy the pink Bible she sleeps with; to Lorrie's adorable granddaughter, Swae, who inspired the scene where Teagan plays the piano for the wedding; to Miss Mandy who team teaches with Cindy and graciously takes the three-year-olds potty. To Pastor Steve and Miss Patti who are the inspiration behind the New Covenant Preschool in Scottsdale, Arizona that I used as the model for New Hope Preschool.

To Charlene Prince, an amazing piano teacher who devotedly encourages children to love music.

Finally, to my son Brian and my adorable grand boys who hosted me in Costa Rica and helped me appreciate the bungalows and Playa Hermosa Beach. But, he still hasn't taught his mother how to surf!

And, to my daughter Dana who really is the director of a Christian preschool, but in Arizona (see above), not California. Thank you, Dana, for agreeing to allow me to feature your children, my beautiful grandchildren, as participants in the wedding party. I hope all my grandchildren will be honored to be part of this story.

Not last, really first in my heart, is my praise and thankfulness to my Lord and Savior Jesus Christ who nudged me every day to write this story. If not for Him, I would have given up in frustration.

PROLOGUE

"Ouch!"

"What?"

"You stepped on my toes."

He said it so matter of factly that Cindy wondered if he was kidding. She looked down at his black patent shoes. Aw, oh. A scuff on the right one. Guess Rob was right. Question was … his fault for not being a good leader or hers for being a bad follower?

"Sorry."

"S'okay." He pulled her closer and she felt her body melt into the warmth of his.

CHAPTER ONE

Cindy dug through the cardboard carton. She pulled out fistfuls of old photographs from over twelve years ago. She dug deeper, hoping to find "the one." Finally, she thought she had it, the black and white one of Rob. How she wished she'd had the money to buy the yearbooks before her own graduation. But, her parents were cash-strapped, and she worked during after school hours as a barista at Starbucks. So, some of those years were lost, at least in photos. It was before everyone had cell phones they could store photos in.

She held the blurry photo up to the light. Was Rob really that handsome then? He looked goofy in the image. But, so did the other guys hugging each other's' shoulders. Must have been taken after a track meet. In those days the date of the photograph was noted on the back. Four years before she had graduated.

She found another photo. *Oh, my gosh, almost forgot he was voted class king. He deserved it, but he is so humble now.* She rubbed her eyes and sat down. She could hardly believe she was dating a former class king of Vista del Mar High School. He had never mentioned it. But, that was so teenage, so juvenile. He was all grown up now. Really grown up.

She'd had a huge crush on Rob when she was only starting into her freshman year. He had never seemed to flaunt his kingship, or any of his academic accolades or sports accomplishments. But, she followed them. She knew.

She threw the photos aside, tossing them haphazardly on her kitchen table. What had happened the other evening at Noelle and Braydon's wedding? Her Candy Cane best friend had married a florist. The owner of the floral shop that was previously contracted to provide the flowers for Noelle's original wedding, the one she cancelled because of her former fiancé Clay's abuse. Last night, almost a year later, was a beautiful event. It was after the ceremony when the couple had been toasted and the small ensemble started to play dance music. That's when Rob gently grasped her hand and led her to the area by the pond at the entrance of the Sherman Gardens. That's when she melted in his arms.

He held her close and started to dance, very slowly. His nose nestled in her ear. The little band was playing that old tune "Someday My Prince Will Come" from Disney's Snow White. The singer was crooning in an old fashioned way. "Cynthia," he whispered hoarsely. Cindy thought her heart would leap out of her bridesmaid's gown as red as the taffeta skirt. She snuggled closer.

Suddenly, the band switched to "Santa, Baby," perfect for this Christmas wedding. But, the faster beat seemed to catch Rob off guard. The song was especially perfect since Braydon the groom had proposed to Noelle in a Santa costume at her parents' Christmas party last year. What a hoot that had been. He had been very authentic, even though everyone knew it was him. Noelle had been so overcome with joy she laughed and cried at the same time. What a memory. She had agreed to be Mrs. Santa supervising elves and answering children's letters to the jolly red-clad elf. In perfect English, using her skills as an English teacher.

Cindy shook her head and laughed softly. "What? What did you say, Rob?"

"I said 'Let's go to the parking lot where we can twirl.'" He looked at her quizzically. "You okay being with me?"

"Oh, yes. Forgive me. I was thinking about how your brother proposed to Noelle last Christmas." She pressed closer to him. "I'm sorry, but it was such a treat to see. Too bad you weren't there. You would have loved it."

Rob nodded, somewhat unenthusiastically. "Braydon always was the melodramatic one, the clever one, the one who always managed to get into some kind of trouble or do something dramatic." He sounded jealous, then clasped her hand again. "So, would you? Like to go to the parking lot where we have more room to dance?"

Cindy nodded, then asked, "Should we? Aren't we supposed to stay with the wedding party? And the guests." She could see he wasn't convinced. He was the Best Man, so shouldn't he be available for the rest of the event?

"I suppose. But, maybe just a few minutes where

there is more space, and," he added with a wink, "where we will be more alone."

Cindy wasn't so sure, but it was hard to deny this man. Like his brother, Braydon the groom, he was handsome, but different. Instead of blue eyes like Braydon's, his were hazel, the kind that turned subtle colors – pale brown, even green sometimes. Depending on the light. His face wasn't sculptured like Braydon's, but it was definitely handsome. Especially graced by that full head of luxurious brown hair. Why was she comparing him? It was hard not to because the brothers were so different in stature and coloring. She had expected Robinson to look like a twin to Braydon. Yet, he never had in high school. Maybe she was having a memory lapse.

She took his offered hand and held up her red taffeta skirt so she wouldn't trip. When they reached the parking lot lined with cars, she realized he was right. There was a huge area in the middle. They danced.

She wasn't sure what song was playing because the music barely drifted that far. But, he lived up to his promise, and they twirled. And twirled more, until she was almost dizzy. It was almost magical. She had never expected this somewhat humble and sometimes shy man to be such a marvelous dancer. Definitely a hidden talent. Until now.

Breathless, she laid her hand on his arm. "Rob, I have to stop." He looked at her with a question in his eyes. "I have to use the bathroom!"

"Oh."

"Sorry. Meet you back at the reception. K?"

He nodded. She raced up the low steps holding her skirt again. He followed slowly.

~

The reception was winding down. It was almost midnight. A few guests had left, leaving empty spaces at the round tables. Suddenly, the band played a loud drum roll. The leader approached the microphone and laughed. "Ladies and gentlemen, it is time. Time for all the fun stuff. The groom will toss the garter, if he can find it, and the bride will toss her bouquet." He looked around and snickered. "All single men form a circle around Braydon."

About twenty men and boys shuffled forward. Cindy pushed Rob who protested. "But, I'm his brother. I shouldn't be there."

"You're single, right? Or, am I mistaken?" She pushed him again. Reluctantly, he tried to fade into the group.

The band did a staccato drum beat. Braydon made a big show of trying to find Noelle's garter. Cindy knew it was below her knee because Noelle was embarrassed even having one. But, being a good sport, she played along. Braydon fumbled and pretended to search for it. Noelle giggled when he lifted the skirt of her gown and stuck his head under. He groped, she kicked. Was she going to kick him in the face, the face under her skirt? Finally, he held a blue garter above his head with an impish grin. He swung it around on a finger. Twenty plus pairs of male hands waved in the air. His eyes locked on one, and he aimed. Right at his brother.

Rob had no choice but to catch it. It practically flew into his hands. His face burned crimson, but he held it tight against his chest. A few of the men moaned, but many clapped him on the back. "Your time, buddy. Congratulations, guy." Cindy grinned.

More drum beats, another announcement. "Now, ladies, form a circle. The bride is going to toss her beautiful bouquet." The announcer stopped. "Oops, sorry. She wants to preserve her real bouquet. But, the one she is going to toss is special. Reach to catch."

Cindy was glad Noelle wouldn't toss the gorgeous bouquet Braydon had designed just for her. However, she noticed the one in Noelle's raised hand was also outstanding. That Braydon. He would be sure every floral offering from Love In Bloom Floral would be beautiful.

Cindy hung back behind the excited group of single girls, mostly teen and college age, and the other four Candy Canes, of course. But, they and she were more mature and didn't jiggle and giggle and act crazy. She raised her arms and waved her hands, more obligatory than really expecting to catch. She was watching Doreen. What a gift it would be for her to catch the flowers. Or, Natalie, who struggled financially with her small independent health club, or Candy, divorced and job seeking. She sought each one with her eyes, hoping for them. Not that catching the proverbial wedding bouquet really held the promise tradition claimed. But, it would be nice for any of them to have the special moment. Where she wondered was Connie? The designer of Noelle's gorgeous wedding gown.

She heard cheers and screams and felt something in her hands. Two girls who she didn't know hugged her fiercely and jostled her. What! She hadn't even tried, but the bouquet of red striped Candy Cane roses was in her hands. She felt her face heat up. How did that happen? Noelle's back was to the group as she flung the bouquet over her head. But, Cindy knew even if she had been facing the group of women, she couldn't have planned it. She was a great swimmer, but a notoriously bad aim in softball and basketball. What did this mean that she had caught the bouquet and Rob the garter?

CHAPTER TWO

*C*indy stared at herself in the mirror. She felt different. Did she look different? Not much. Maybe a little flushed. She brushed the sides of her long hair back with her fingers to the top of her head. She did look different that way, maybe more sophisticated? Holding the bulk of hair at her crown she grinned in the glass. After all, that was the way her tresses had been for her bridesmaid attire. And the diamond studs Noelle had lent her for her ears made her look older, more worldly. Was Rob attracted to her because of her appearance? After all, she is at least four years younger than he, maybe close to five. But, didn't most men like younger women?

She released the clumps of brown hair letting them fall around her neck. Rob didn't seem the phony type. In fact, he did seem a tad shy. However, he was the one to suggest dancing in the parking lot so they could twirl and be more alone. Go figure. *Men will always be a mystery to me.*

She smeared on night cream, pulled on her flannel jammies, said her prayers and flopped into bed. The post wedding brunch started at ten tomorrow. As a bridal attendant, she needed to be on time at the Newport Marriott. Noelle had a thing about punctuality.

~

"Yes. I guess I will help you." Cindy looked askance at Rob. "What will I have to do?"

She was flattered Rob asked her to be Mrs. Santa at Love In Bloom Floral Shop since he'd agreed to take over for Braydon while he was on his honeymoon with Noelle. It was out of her league, but he expected her to show up tomorrow at nine. The shop didn't open until ten, but apparently there was a lot to get ready.

Cindy was used to tiny children and overly concerned parents. Teaching the three year olds at New Hope Preschool was a gift. She didn't make a lot in money, but she made a lot in relationships. All the teachers and staff were Christian, so they supported each other in prayer and friendship. Ms. Dana the director was a gift to all of them. Cindy knew she had her own challenges raising four children alone, but she always stepped up to the plate to support her staff. She was also very skilled at comforting parents who had concerns, and especially skilled at dealing with tiny boys and girls crying and wetting pants and acting out physically. (He hit me first!) Yes, being a preschool teacher at New Hope was a challenge, and a gift.

She thought about how Miss Lorrie, Ms. Dana's sidekick and alter ego, was a hero to all the little children. She went to every classroom every morning and taught the Bible in a way even the youngest little ones could understand. One of Ms. Dana's own children, a twin, who had "graduated" two years ago from the preschool Kindergarten class, still went to sleep holding her Bible every night, the one Miss Lorrie had given her. Sometimes, she held her teddy bear, too. Still, it was a testimony to the school and the influence it had.

Rob opened the door for her and handed her a Santa hat. Glad she had worn her black tights and new red sweater. She perched the silly hat on her head, shoving curls under it haphazardly and smiled weakly.

~

"Welcome ... Mrs. Santa!" His face beamed that engaging grin. Cindy grinned back and fussed with tucking her curls under the red tassel hat. "Put me to work before I change my mind."

He showed her how to arrange groups of flowers in the cool case, and she started having fun. They all smelled so wonderful.

"Do you mind if I get a bit creative?"

"Help yourself. Go for it.," he declared.

She added candy canes and lollipops on sticks to several arrangements. Even a glittery butterfly on a long stick to one. Braydon had a drawer full of fun trimmings. After adding the decorations, she went to the computer and printed out several new descriptions to add. Finally, she made new banners to put in the window.

She was taping them up, forward facing, so passersby couldn't miss them, when the door burst open and a strong female voice startled her.

"What does this mean? What does Buy One get One Half Off and Get a Coupon for Valentine's Day mean?"

"Oh, Mrs. Lovejoy, how lovely to see you." Cindy quivered, realized her knees were knocking. What had she done wrong?

"Nice to see you, too, Cynthia." She had used Cindy's formal name. Indicating what?

"So kind of you to help Robinson." Mrs. Lovejoy paused focusing on Rob and Cindy. "Was the idea his, yours, or both of yours? The promotion, I mean."

Cindy bumped her two quivering knees together to steady them, then stood up straight. "I guess mine," she admitted. "But, I did run it past Rob."

"I see," the older woman said in a placating voice. "Still, I wish to be informed when we have specials or sales." She fumbled in her purse and drew out a tissue. "I guess I'm a bit overwrought. Wedding, you know." She dabbed at her eyes, finally smiled. "Sorry, Cindy," she said, finally using the woman's nickname like everyone else. "Guess I over-reacted."

Cindy reached both hands toward Rob's mother. "I didn't mean to overstep, but wanted to draw attention to the shop. Especially during the Christmas season."

"I'm sorry, too. I did over-react." She touched Cindy's hands delicately. Searching Cindy's face, she grinned widely and hugged the startled woman.

"You helping Rob is a gift. Thank you so much. I trust you both to make good decisions."

After Mrs. Lovejoy left, Cindy wondered about that comment.

CHAPTER THREE

*R*ob swung the double doors open at precisely ten. A gust of cool air swooshed through the shop, and some of the premade bouquets shimmered. Cindy raised her brows in question and reached for her sweater. December in Southern California wasn't bitter cold, but there was a chill in the air. Still, open doors were more inviting.

"Cold?" Rob asked.

"A bit. But, I do think people have more of a tendency to come into an open door shop. Less intimidating. And, they can more easily see the beautiful flowers."

He nodded and stepped behind the counter to the cutting table beyond the archway. Grabbing a clump of baby's breath he started to cut the bottoms of the woody stems with a big knife. "Let's leave the doors open for a little while. But, if you get too cold, we'll close them."

"Oops. We almost forgot this." Cindy rolled out the little wrought iron cart and angled it near the doors on the sidewalk. It was filled with small urns of various flowers, hopefully tempting passersby to stop and admire. She had placed little flag signs on long skewers in each bunch with prices and BUY A BUNCH, GET A BUNCH HALF OFF. A narrow banner across the side of the French-style cart said HOLIDAY SPECIALS. She hoped the cart and its presentations would attract attention.

Suddenly, voices started to sing loudly, and off key. "We wish you a Merry Christmas." Candy, Natalie, Connie and Doreen, even Melanie, crowded through the doors and giggled jostling each other.

Cindy was stunned. She grinned at all the Candy Canes and grasped Melanie's hands. "What are you doing here with these crazy girls?" She didn't mean it as a criticism, but she was surprised. Even though all the girls liked her, they usually didn't include an outsider. But, Cindy wondered, was she one? Noelle had included her as a bridesmaid.

"I," Melanie pronounced, "am now an honorary Candy Cane." She searched Cindy's face. "You okay with that?"

Cindy wasn't sure how to respond. But, Melanie, who had caused Doreen's accident was totally forgiven, and she had loosely become one of the group. Who, she wondered, had made *that* decision. Not her, and she was the group leader.

"In case you are wondering," Melanie said, "they put me through the paces. I had to swim ten laps to qualify." She raised a radiant face to Cindy. "I am SO proud."

Cindy swallowed the lump in her throat, hard. Melanie was a sincere woman who had made a mistake, one that changed the life of another. Forever. Yet, Cindy reminded herself, Melanie was God's child and had embraced the Candy Canes as good friends. She stepped forward and threw her arms around Melanie's soft frame.

"I am proud of you, too," she said. "Welcome to the group. Oops, I mussed up your hair."

Melanie laughed her signature tinkling laugh. "Not a big deal. I think it's still damp from the pool." She looked intently at Cindy. "Did I tell you we just came from there?"

"So that's why I couldn't get in touch with any of you this morning."

"Oh," Connie spoke up. "We all had our phones on silent. Guess we never checked our messages." She looked around the group. "Did anyone?" They all shook their heads.

"Well, I'm glad everyone's okay," Cindy exclaimed. "And, you have good news."

She gestured toward the workroom with her chin. "Rob, come out and see who's here."

Rob came from the back of the shop's workroom wearing his apron, the beige heavy cotton one to protect his clothing from flying cut stems and the chemicals in preservatives.

Cindy thought every Candy Cane's eyes bulged. What? They had all met him at Noelle's and Braydon's wedding. After all, he had been the Best Man.

They were acting like silly nellies, whispering among themselves like star struck teenagers. Were these women all really mid-twenties? She felt her cheeks heat up in
embarrassment. Just as she was about to shush them,

she heard a cacophony of giggles.

Rob was bowing, sweeping one arm dramatically in front of him. "Ladies," he said in a hoarse whisper, "I am honored by your presence."

He turned to a bouquet of roses and one by one plucked a blossom out, handed one to each woman in turn with a bow that graced his handsome face with that beautiful smile that Cindy adored. She thought she would pass out.

~

Rob closed the double glass doors at seven. Cindy had pulled the flower cart back inside and was turning off the lights in the workroom. They had dimmed the lights in the glass flower cases, checked the temperature in the room and wiped off the counters.

"All set?" He scanned Cindy's face noticing it seemed a little pinched. Maybe from the chilly weather? Or, was she upset about something? They hadn't talked much after the Candy Canes left; there had been so much to do, and thankfully several customers came in to buy bouquets. One, sadly, to order a funeral wreath. He would deliver that tomorrow. Devastating right before Christmas to lose a loved one.

"Wanna grab a coffee?" He knew she loved Starbucks' Frappuccinos, or was it too cold for that? Still, the coffee house was only a block away, and they could walk. He refused to drive there. At this time of evening, actually any time, parking would be a ridiculous waste, an endeavor in futility. Corona del Mar's nightlife woke up at sundown, especially a few days before Christmas. And both his car and the delivery van were safely ensconced behind the store.

Cindy's eyes looked a little wet. The weather?

Chilly weather often affected his latent allergies, and his muscles. Maybe hers, too. She bundled up in her heavy sweater, pulled its collar up to her neck and merely whispering "No, thanks" scooted out the door almost slipping on the damp pavement. The rain had started in sprinkles around five. Now, it was steady. He watched Cindy pull her sweater up over her head. No umbrella. But, neither of them would have predicted, neither watched or heard the weather report that morning. Who had time?

On impulse, he wasn't sure why, he raced after her. Yelling. "Wait! Wait, Cindy, please."

She didn't stop. Maybe she couldn't hear him with the hustle bustle sounds of traffic and the sudden thunder. Maybe she could. Maybe that's why she started to run. She was so far ahead he couldn't catch up with her. He turned around and slopped through puddles back to the shop.

Rob felt like a heel.

CHAPTER FOUR

Why was everything in her life so complicated? Especially romance. Especially now Rob. Had she misread his intentions, the cues he'd given her during that special parking lot dance? Yes, she'd heard his voice calling after her when she left the floral shop, and she picked up her pace. Maybe she should have slowed down, turned around. Would he have wrapped her in his arms? Now, she would never know, only dream.

Cindy reached her parked car several blocks away. That morning she had felt blessed to grab a spot in the alley behind the businesses lining Pacific Coast Highway. Now, she was sorry she hadn't paid for parking nearer to the floral shop. It would have been a stretch financially, especially for the whole day, but so worth it not to be dripping drenched. She did a dog shake, like she'd seen Noelle's little dog Misty do to shake the water off her coat, then slipped into her car.

What? The motor wouldn't turn over. Drat! She tried again, even letting it settle for a few minutes. But, each time she turned the key, she heard a growling rrrr sound. Not good.

She pulled her cell phone out of her coat pocket. She didn't belong to AAA. But, she did belong to the Candy Canes. Maybe one of them could help.

~

Rob mopped his wet hair with a towel normally used to clean up floral messes. What had he done wrong? He knew his offer for coffee was rather flip. Not very personal. He had never thanked Cindy for all her work today, either. He had taken it for granted.

When her friends came in he'd had so much fun. Normally, he wasn't demonstrative like his brother Braydon. Maybe God was saying for him to break out of his shell. Be courageous. He'd had no trouble in high school and college participating in sports, even excelling in track. But, girls, women …

He should have trusted his legs to run faster, harder to keep up with her. He opened an umbrella that Braydon kept by the door and tried to remember where Cindy had taken off to.

~

Cindy wept. Had all those silly girls still kept their phones on silent? Even her text messages didn't go through. Just as she was about to leave her car and walk the three miles home, she heard a voice calling her name. Rob?

"Cindy, Cindy," he yelled. His voice echoed. "Where are you? Are you safe? Turn on your headlights so I can find you."

She tried. Didn't work. Tried again. Finally, she got out of her car holding the flashlight she kept in the glove compartment. Its beam was weak, but it was something. She waved it around.

She felt strong arms around her, squeezing her tight. Because she couldn't see in the dim light she really hoped it was Rob.

CHAPTER FIVE

"So, Mr. Gorgeous rescued you?"

The Candy Canes were all assembled in Kerstin Day's living room. As tradition, she was having her pre-Christmas party with soup and corn muffins and ornament exchange. Noelle and Braydon wouldn't be there this time. They were on their honeymoon in Hawaii, but everyone felt their love and blessings. They would be back for Christmas Day.

Cindy looked at Candace. Was she the one who spoke? Sometimes, it was hard to tell since the girls were so close for so many years. Their voices blended together.

"If you mean Rob," she hesitated, "Lovejoy. Yes." She paused and looked around the small group nestled together on the sofa. "He was my temporary hero. Yes, he used his AAA membership to have my car towed and a new battery put in."

Everyone grinned, and there was a lot of throat clearing, but no one responded.

~

What had he done? Or, rather, what hadn't he? Rob crossed his ankles on the coffee table and stared into the fire, the fake one with a fake, pre-pressed log covered in glossy printed paper. The one he'd used was designated 3 Hours. It should last until more than eleven since he put it on about eight or so, after he got back from helping Cindy with her car problem.

The Triple A guy said it was probably not just the battery, maybe the alternator. Much bigger problem, much more expense. Could she, he wondered, afford the repairs? Probably not on her preschool teaching salary. Hadn't anyone advised her about car stuff? A brother, father, uncle, the pastor at the preschool? He didn't know much about Cindy, about whether she had family in the area, or at all.

Of course he, actually Braydon, was paying her for working at the floral shop during the Christmas break when school was closed. He hated to disturb Bray on his honeymoon, but he thought his brother wouldn't mind a quick text, especially since Cindy was a Candy Cane and Braydon had married one. Laughing under his breath to himself, he typed a fast message asking Bray to be generous to Cindy.

> Girl might need some financial help. Major car probs. Pay her generously? Hope you two are having a great time in Maui. Aloha!

Return text came back immediately.

> Yes. Pay generously. Checkbook is in second drawer on left in main counter. You are on the account. Will pray. What else can we do to help?

Having fun! Aloha!

What were the honeymooners doing? Hopefully, having a scrumptious dinner of exotic seafood. Wow, he was on the account? Braydon was always full of surprises.

~

Rob unlocked the door of the floral shop fifteen minutes early. He wanted to be sure to find that checkbook. The honeymooners would be back in a couple of days with plans to open the shop the day after Christmas in time for New Year's orders.

Cindy bounced in smiling just minutes before ten. She always made him feel so upbeat. Her cute grin was like a happy nudge. What a great way to start the day, just two days before Christmas.

"Good morning, Robinson! Today is going to be great. Dontcha think?" She cocked her head and bumped his chin with a delicate fist. Were those sparkles on her fingertips?

Grabbing her right hand he swung her around, then held her close. He pushed the button for the overhead music and started to dance. "We have three minutes. Let's do it."

"Whoa, Mr. Lovejoy, is this part of the deal?" She tilted her head again and her eyes shined back to his. "You must be happy to be finishing this gig." Her laughter filled the space and almost shimmied a few bouquets. Rob ignored one about to fall.

"Not really. It's been a nice break from routine." He paused as if measuring his words. "I enjoy working with you. I especially enjoy dancing with you." There, he'd said it. His words almost caught in his throat.

Something about this woman ... Was it trust? Definitely curiosity. She always seemed happy, and made those around her happy. What would she do if she knew his secrets? How would she react? With disdain? Probably. He shoved the thought aside, deep into his gut, and twirled her – just as the bell jingled announcing a customer.

A woman with streaks of gray in her short hair stood just inside the door grinning. "How delightful! Entertainment. Do you two dance professionally?"

Cindy released herself from Rob's arms. "Not really. It's just such a happy season." Reaching a hand to the woman, she introduced herself and said, "I'm Cindy. And, this is Rob Lovejoy, proprietor. Welcome to the shop. How can we help you?"

"I, uh, wondered if Braydon is here?"

"Oh, he's on his honeymoon ... in Hawaii." Her voice lilted in joy.

"He got married?" The woman looked at both of them and actually hooted. "So happy for him. About time." She said. "Tell me all about it." So, they did.

~

Rob bit his lip. He was cutting woody, thick rose stems when the knife slipped. Blood trickled onto the counter. How stupid, and it hurt. He grabbed a tissue and pressed it hard against the cut. It was a clean cut, almost like a paper cut. Sharp, from a well-honed knife. Almost made him laugh at his slipup, which he hoped it literally was. His right hand holding the knife shook a little. That was normal, wasn't it? But, normal wasn't a part of him anymore.

He reached in the overhead cabinet for a box of band aids and burst out laughing. There were three boxes. One was Spider Man, one Disney princesses, one Super Heroes. All had cute graphic pictures on them. Not one was a normal, generic band aid. Leave it to Braydon and his sense of humor. Oh, well, better a Super Hero than nothing. He pulled one out and tried to apply it, but doing it with one hand was almost impossible. The shop was quiet, and for once he was glad it wasn't crowded with customers.

"Cindy?" he yelled. "Can you help?"

She came running, and gasped.

CHAPTER SIX

"*O*h, my gosh! What happened?" She stared at the red pool on the wood counter. Then, the knife. Both counter and knife had more than traces of blood on them. Very red blood.

But, she reminded herself, wasn't most blood red? Duh, Cindy. Jump into the moment to help.

She grabbed a paper towel from the spool and started to mop up the blood on the knife and butcher block when she heard Rob growl, sort of.

"Cindy, I need you to help me. Not wipe off the counter." He sounded almost angry. In the millisecond her brain started to operate again, she spun toward him. She was usually good in emergencies. Hadn't she been the one who made all the calls to the Candy Canes and gathered them all at the hospital during Doreen's accident? She was the one they called strong, the leader of the group. But, this was Rob who made her knees weak, who danced like a dream, who she was starting to care for … maybe more than she should.

"I'm s-s- sorry. I guess I misunderstood. I thought you wanted me to clean up." She clasped her hands at her waist and peeked at his face. It was blank. Hadn't he just asked for her help? Finally, she noticed his hands gripped together and held out away from his body. The tissue he held against one was soaked in red.

"I need you to put a band aid on this silly cut I got." He looked at her curiously. "I know it's a strange request, but I need to stop the bleeding."

Cindy nodded and looked at the array of band aid boxes on the shelf. "Okay, big man." Was that an appropriate inference? She meant it jokingly, but his brow furrowed at the jest. "No offense. Just giving you your due." She prayed a few phrases from Proverbs 16 to keep her errant mouth shut. But, she reminded herself, he really is a big man. In her eyes, at least.

"So, you wanna be a Super Hero, a Disney princess or Spider Man?" She couldn't resist teasing. He looked so devastated and vulnerable, like a ten-year-old kid. Really, it was just a cut.

"I'll take Spidey. Still my fav at my age." He chuckled, and Cindy felt much better.

She pulled two Spider Man embellished band aids out of the appropriate box, opened the seals around them and held them out. Pressing them hard onto Rob's finger, he grinned.

"Perfect. You got it. Thanks." He squeezed her hand with this unbandaged one. "I think it's going to work."

Cindy nodded and retreated to the shop when she heard the bell ring. She was relieved. She might be strong in some ways, but she was no nurse.

~

Rob wandered out holding several bunches of Braydon's famous Candy Cane roses. "I stripped them of thorns and removed all the bottom leaves." He handed them to Cindy who immediately put them in funnel-shaped containers and nestled them in the cool case.

"Even though it's just two days before Christmas, they should sell well. We can wrap them with a few real candy canes, like extra embellishments." She sounded so delighted with the idea. "I'll put a Candy Cane Roses banner in the window."

"You have learned so much, just helping here for the past week." His voice was warm, and he took her hand.

"Thanks, Rob. I've enjoyed every minute. Except the bloody part." She laughed self-consciously. "So, what about tomorrow? It's Christmas Eve." She cocked her head, begging the question. "I assume we are open. But, until when? What time?"

Rob looked all around the shop ... at the cool case stocked with pre-grouped bunches of flowers, at the enticing arrangements on the rounders, and the shelf that held all the beautiful vases customers could purchase. Finally, he stopped at the huge Christmas tree. It was decorated in silk flowers and little parchment ornaments with Bible verses printed on them. And, lots of angels – every kind and shape, but all exquisite in tulle and lace and taffeta with wings made of feathers.

"I think Bray used to close the shop by five on Christmas Eve." He felt a little confused. He put a hand on his forehead and said, "I should call Mom and ask her." He felt so out of it. Was it the disease causing the confusion? Why couldn't he make a decision? He knew Braydon left a list of instructions, but where were they? He hated the ambivalence. Why couldn't he remember?

Cindy looked at him with a strange expression. He noticed one eyebrow was cocked up higher than the other, and her cute nose was wrinkled, the tip poking up. "You okay?," she asked.

"Yep, fine." He smiled at her, hoping it was reassuring. "Just trying to remember the routine."

"That's understandable, considering you've never done this before so close to Christmas."

She was right, and her comment made him feel so much better. So much so, that he took a risk. "Do you have plans for tomorrow night, for Christmas Eve?" He searched her face again, hoping she would say no. "I can't remember," he blabbed on without thinking, "if you have family here in town ... to spend it with, I mean."

She shook her head. "No. Not for a long time. Family is in Omaha." She paused. "Since my mom died, we try to do our get-togethers later in the year, in the spring. Airfares are cheaper then, as well as hotels." She stopped to chuckle. "At least there they are. Not in Newport. Gotta go to the Midwest during winter, sort of like a reverse Snowbird." He laughed at that. What a concept.

"I love it! Reverse Snowbird. Too funny."

Getting up his courage, he decided to risk it. Just ask her. Maybe she already had plans with friends, with the other Candy Canes. He blurted it out.

"Mom and Dad always do a special Christmas Eve thing. Of course, Bray and Noelle will probably opt out since they will just be arriving from their honeymoon.

CINDY'S PERFECT DANCE

But," he hesitated, "would you like to come? You would be very welcome," he added. And waited for her response.

~

Cindy was thrilled to be asked to join the Lovejoys. She'd had no plans, just the early Christmas Eve church service and pizza. Not that she cared what she ate, but being with special people ... well, she couldn't imagine. Did he really want her?

She didn't want to seem so enthusiastic that she seemed desperate. Maybe he felt sorry for her; or, maybe he had a special, longtime girlfriend who'd been out of town before Christmas, before Rob and she managed the floral shop, before they'd danced at the wedding. Would she walk into the Lovejoy's living room and see another woman sitting beside him?

"Uh, that's very nice, Rob. But, I don't know." She found herself looking at his chin. "Maybe your parents would rather keep it family. I don't want to intrude." Or, be the odd man out she thought to herself. That would be horrible, and uncomfortable. No, unbearable.

He looked her square in the face and grasped her hands. "Do you really think I would ask you that way? Like not part of the family?

"You," he emphasized the noun, "ARE part of the family. You are a Candy Cane, right?"

Cindy laughed with him. Being one of six, now seven with Melanie included, did make them special. "Okay. If you are sure. I would love to join you all.

"Oh, Rob, what about your mom? She is the hostess, it is her home. I'm sure she has special plans."

Cindy had never heard such a guffaw of laughter. What had gotten into Rob? He was holding his belly

35

and almost doubled over. "What?"

"*What* is right!" he said. "My parents' home is totally and always open, especially at Christmas." He looked at her again and laughed … again. But, not so effusively. "You wanna come?" He paused to give her time to respond. Should she accept? What would being with the whole Lovejoy family mean?

CHAPTER SEVEN

*C*indy pulled her now repaired little car up to the Lovejoy's house and parked in front on the street. There must have been ten other cars there. Surely they were at neighboring homes. Rob said this was a family gathering. She trotted to the door holding a small hostess gift, one her granny had often given.

Mrs. Day opened the door. No staff? How nice. She was surprised, had expected a server in fancy black and white uniform. But, what was Noelle's mother doing here?

Mrs. Day answered her unspoken question. "Lydia appointed me door opener," she laughed heartily as she said it. "Welcome. Come in and join this crazy group."

Mrs. Lovejoy stepped forward and grasped Cindy's hand. She felt more relaxed around Rob's mother than the other day in the shop. She figured it was only natural the Lovejoys and Days would become friends since their children had recently married each other. She was enveloped in a hug and a whiff of delicate perfume.

"Where should I put this little gift I brought?"

"Oh, let me take it." Mrs. Lovejoy said. "There is a designated pile in the guest bedroom." She grinned and took the small package from Cindy. "Unless it is something that should be included in tonight's festivities?" She tilted her head to question Cindy. "And, please, Cindy … may I call you that? … Please call me Lydia." Cindy smiled.

"I know," Lydia said, "accidental alliteration when I married." She laughed again, and Cindy thought her voice charming.

"Uh, … Lydia," Cindy had trouble calling Rob's mother by her first name, but she stammered on. "What exactly are tonight's festivities?" She looked at the other woman's face for a clue. "Was I supposed to contribute in some way? Rob never said."

"*So* Rob." Lydia's face twisted in frustration. Finally, she said more. "He is a bit reticent about sharing. Even at his age." She sighed, rather loudly Cindy thought. "It's a trust issue." Then she took Cindy's little hostess gift and disappeared. Into the guest bedroom? Hopefully, her glass Bluebird of Happiness would be added to the pile.

~

Rob was glad Cindy came, but he was nervous about introducing her to his special pals. Thank goodness some of the Candy Canes were here. At least she'd have some familiar faces to chat with. He stretched his arms forward to take her small hands in his big ones and led her into the melee. When she saw Doreen and Candy he could almost feel her relax. The three women started chatting together. Doreen looked him full in the face. "How do you know all these people, Rob? Obviously, they are friends of yours." She paused. "From some kind of business group?"

He knew the CCs, as he had privately dubbed them, were aware he was a real estate entrepreneur. Most of them also knew he surfed. Yes, either explanation would do. "Yes, some are. We realtors have a loose, but wide, association," he said. He hoped that would explain. After all, it seemed lately that the meetings he attended were dominated by realtors and others connected to the industry." He nodded toward two men, one with longish hair laughing together. "Brad and Nick are surfing buddies, and Nick is a loan officer who specializes in mortgages." There, that should be explanation enough. He excused himself to help his dad pull some of the living room furniture in a circle.

Candy leaned in close to Cindy. "Do you know what is going on? Why the set-up?"

"Maybe we're going to sing carols? Or watch Scrooge on that big screen TV." Cindy pointed to the large black screen above the fireplace mantle. "After all, it is Christmas Eve."

Rob overheard their not very well concealed whispering. Won't they be surprised!

"Ladies, come join us and take a seat." He waved his arm toward the loose circle of chairs on either side of the deep sofa. The girls shrugged at each other and did as he asked.

~

Candy and Doreen searched for seats. Both held plastic glasses of bubbly red liquid. Just as they were about to split up, Rob's two surfer friends stood up. The one called Nick moved over leaving two empty spots on the sofa between Brad and himself. "Over here, lovely ladies." He pointed with a long finger to the empty space. The girls blushed a little, Cindy noticed, but they settled between the two men. Very handsome men she thought.

Surely Rob had saved a place for her. But, when she looked around, he was sitting on a barstool behind Noelle's dad, close to the fireplace. Darrell Day held a big open book on his knees, and Rob's dad Logan held what looked like a video camera. Kerstin Day and Lydia Lovejoy stood off to the side holding piles of clothing. What were they doing?

She spied a chair, the only empty one, between two women about her age. Well, maybe time to make new friends. "May I join you?" Cindy wasn't sure why she asked since there was no other place to sit.

"Please do," the brunette with the short bob said kindly. The other girl with dangly earrings imitating Christmas wreaths that seemed to catch strands of her shoulder length blonde hair when she turned her face to Cindy, said, "This will be fun. Rob mentioned this at the meeting the other night." She tapped jiggling knees with brilliantly red manicured nails. Mmm. Nervous girl.

"Oh, a realtors' meeting?" Cindy asked. "So close to Christmas?"

Blonde raised her eyebrows over a blank face. Cindy felt the other girl's arm slip behind her and rest on the top of her chair back. Was she tapping Blondie on the shoulder? In her peripheral vision she could swear the dark haired girl shook her head slightly. She was just about to ask if they wanted to sit next to each other when Darrell Day cleared his throat loudly. Cindy noticed a guitar was perched across Rob's left knee. He started strumming softly. When all the guests had quieted down, he broke into Silent Night, and everyone started singing.

She had guessed right. What a great way to celebrate Christmas Eve. They only sang the first verse. Probably because without the prompts most churches gave on big screens, few remembered more. When the final "heavenly peace" was sung, Kerstin Day rang a bell. Cindy noticed it was the kind most people associate with hanging around a reindeer neck. Cute. When the chuckling and giggling died down and she had everyone's attention, she made a quiet announcement. "Does anyone know what's coming next? Any guesses?" Lydia held up the pile of clothing in her arms; Kerstin did, too. Grinning impishly she stepped forward and finally spoke. "This was my idea, actually my family's. Something we've done for years since our boys were little." She glanced at Rob who nodded, but whose face took on Christmas color. "Kerstin and Darrell were kind and generous to allow us to go along with it tonight."

"Please," she continued, "feel under the front of your chairs." She waited while everyone did as instructed. A few came up with post-it notes in their hands and waved them. "Great. Did anyone get a star?"

Cindy raised her hand with the star post-it in it wondering what on earth that meant.

"Cindy!" Lydia sounded excited. "You are the star." She paused to search for Cindy's reaction. "If you are willing."

Cindy nodded, hoping this would be fun. As it

turned out, it was more than special.

~

Rob held her hand as he led her back to her car. She held a beautiful devotional book nestled in tissue in a colorful holiday bag in one hand and squeezed his big warm one with the other. She started to slip into the driver's side of her car when he pulled her close.

"I was honored you got the role of Mary in the family play." He said. "I wondered if the moms had planned it." He looked at her askew. "Did you mind?"

"Mind? No, I loved it. Ever since I was ten I wanted to play Virgin Mary in the church program." She smiled at him. "Had to wait a few years, but it was awesome.

"I hope your mothers didn't 'plan it' for me to be Mary." It was almost a question. Did he know?

"Not that I know." He looked into her eyes. Cindy thought she could drown in their pools.

~

Cindy and Rob had agreed to meet at the floral shop at eight, even though it was Christmas Day. Just for a quick cleanup and reconnoiter. They doubted anyone would come to purchase today, but they had so much to do the next day taking down the Christmas tree, it would be good to get a head start. After checking there was water in all the pre-assembled bouquets and discarding any drooping flowers, they were about to close shop and lock the doors when a distraught looking young man burst in.

"Oh, please, please," he pleaded. "Are you really open?"

"Not exactly," Rob said. "But, what do you need?"

"She finally agreed to marry me. Last night. On

Christmas Eve." His blue eyes were moist and his tousled dark curls showed evidence of hands running through them. He searched Cindy and Rob's faces and apparently decided to trust them. "She invited me for Christmas dinner," he explained in a breathless voice. "I need to bring something special to her and to her mother. Can you help?"

"Can we!" Rob proclaimed. "You bet.

"Cindy, can you gather some Christmas roses?" He turned to her with a devilish smile.

"Of course. Coming right up." She grinned. "We aren't called Love in Bloom for nothing."

Together, Rob and Cindy wrapped two gorgeous bouquets in Cellophane and embellished with candy canes and lots of bows. They thought the young man might collapse he was so overwhelmed when they refused to charge him.

"That was special!" Cindy gazed into Rob's eyes.

"Yep." He looked back into hers. "Christmas." Was all he said.

CHAPTER EIGHT

"*That* was something special." Rob opened his arms to Cindy.

She nodded, hesitated and stepped forward. It was hard to resist the warmth of his arms, when she wanted them so badly, especially on Christmas. He wrapped his large arms around her in a comforting hug.

When he nibbled her ear, she almost collapsed. Then, she giggled.

"Rob!" She cried. "Are you sure about this display of affection?"

"Oh, very sure." He grinned that lopsided grin that shook her heart. Flutters, surely from her heart, floated up to her throat almost choking her. She petitioned her creator. *What, God, was that about?*

"I'd better go." Cindy pulled away from Rob and reached to grab her purse.

"Really? Do you have to?" Rob's hands were still on her shoulders. "I was hoping we could spend at least part of Christmas together." He cocked his head, questioning.

"Uh. Don't you have to spend it with your parents? And, aren't Braydon and Noelle coming home today?"

"Yes. I offered to pick them up at the airport, but they insisted they are taking a shuttle." He cleared his throat, rather dramatically Cindy thought. "I don't suppose they need to see me when they step off the plane."

"I guess, even though you were the best man, they would want to see your parents first. Or, the Days."

Rob's hands slipped gently down from her shoulders to her fingers. She automatically squeezed them. What on earth was she doing? Making it harder to let go and say goodbye.

Her mouth took over like a squawking Myna bird. Sounded like one, too. "Nachos? You like Nachos?"

"Yum. Love them. You offering?"

She wiggled her eye brows, grabbed her purse and led him to the door. "My famous ones," she declared. "Follow me. In your own car," she added over her shoulder with a grin.

~

Rob settled on the velour suede red sofa, pushed a throw pillow behind him and asked, "What makes your Nachos so special?"

Cindy had insisted he plunk down there while she did her Nacho thing. He liked the ambiance, the contemporary décor. Simple, clean, uncluttered. Like Cindy, he thought.

"Want a glass of wine while I mix up the Nachos?" He could hear Cindy popping a cork.

"No thanks. Not tonight, anyway."

"That's okay. You mind if I have one?"

"Not at all. Go for it."

"Soft drink?"

"Sure."

"Pepsi? Coke? Sprite?"

"Any will do." He sucked in a deep breath. Maybe it was time. Especially if their relationship was to go anywhere. Time to be honest, confess.

She set a Pepsi in a glass filled with cracked ice before him on the coffee table.

"You okay, Rob? You look a little strange."

"Yes, and no." He clasped her hand and pulled her down next to him on the sofa. "Something I need to tell you, probably should have some time ago."

"Something bad?"

"Depends on how you understand it."

Cindy nodded and clasped his hand tighter. The look on his face frightened her.

~

Rob is an alcoholic!

The next morning Cindy still couldn't get her mind around it. She didn't know much about the situation, or as Rob said, "the disease." He explained, and after he left, she googled. He made it very clear that if their relationship (was there one?) continued, there should be no pressure on her. She could have a glass of wine or a beer or even a cocktail anytime. At home, or out on a date. He was covered. Her drinking would have no effect on him.

She called Candy.

~

"What are you asking me?" Candy.

"I'm not sure, really. I know you had a breakup with your ex, and you were secretive about why."

Cindy paused. "I don't want to put you on the spot, but maybe you can help me."

"Like how?"

"I probably shouldn't have bothered you. Sorry."

"No, Cindy, don't hang up."

"You sure? This could get personal."

"That's okay. Maybe about time I shared." Cindy heard Candy take a whooshing breath.

"All right. I will ask bluntly. Point blank." She held the phone receiver so tight her knuckles ached.

"Why did you and Dev break up? You seemed so happy."

The whooshing breath echoed over the phone again. "He was a drunk."

"And …"

"I assume there was a question mark after that comment."

Cindy wasn't sure if Candy's remark was a question or a statement. "Yeh. I guess.

"As I said, none of my beeswax. Just trying to figure out something."

"Let me tell you a story," Candy said.

~

Cindy put down the phone and fiddled with her fingers, then held her forehead in her hands, then fiddled with her fingers. She hated knowing other peoples' secrets. But, now that she did, what should she do with them? Obviously, honor and protect them. But, Candy wanted her to learn from her experience, and Rob wanted her support.

Cindy adored Candy, maybe more than the other Candy Canes. She had a strange combination of vulnerability and strength. Must be what she went through with her marriage, and divorce. Maybe made her stronger than the other girls.

Why had Rob shared with her? How would her knowledge affect their relationship? Bigger question, is there a relationship?

On impulse she dialed.

CHAPTER NINE

"Rob, we need to talk."

"I agree. Coffee at Starbucks?"

"Twenty minutes?"

They squeezed into a corner booth. She always thought of corner booths as being cozy. This one felt like a mini battlefield. Rob reached for her hand, and she pulled it away tucking it tightly in its companion. She lowered her eyes to avoid looking at the crushed expression on his face. What was wrong with her? She probably knew a dozen people who were alcoholics, just didn't know that about them. But, this was Rob who made her heart beat erratically and her palms sweat. The man who was close to becoming "her Rob." Could he be, ever? Would she always be testing his breath with her kisses? Would he expect her to abstain, too? No, she couldn't live in that uncertainty.

Rob blinked rapidly. He hugged his arms across his chest. "Well?" When Cindy didn't look up, he said, "You afraid to look at me? I'm still me; same old Rob, not some monster."

She shook her head. "I don't know what to think. I'm scared."

"That's normal," he said.

She cocked her head and raised her eyebrows. "Really?"

"Cindy, I wouldn't expect you to dance in the streets having learned about my health history." He leaned forward placing his hands on the table across from her. "If you were blasé or cavalier about my alcoholic background ... notice I said "background," not current condition ... I would think you didn't take what I told you seriously. And," he continued, "I would think you were being flip."

She felt her nose drip and her cheeks heat up. "You're right. It's because I care for you. I'm scared of the future." She looked at the dimple in his chin. How she would love to wake up to that every morning. Grabbing a crumbled tissue from her purse she swiped at her nose. "Please, tell me all so I understand better."

"Not here. People are starting to give us dirty looks for sitting at this table so long." He grinned and offered a hand to help her up. "Can we go to your place? Maybe for Nachos?"

~

Cindy chopped tomatoes, minced green onions, opened a can of sliced black olives, cut up a fresh avocado and spayed it with lime juice, grated two cheeses and crumbled another, then set them aside. She spritzed cooking spray on a big round white platter, loaded it with her wonderful new find of $2 Only brand tortilla chips and sprinkled all the other ingredients on top. Rob kissed her neck, and she swatted him away.

"Not fair at all!"

"Sorry, but since you wouldn't let me have a chip, I had to taste something yummy."

How could she not giggle? He was so adorable. And, he danced like a dream.

She put the platter of Nachos in the microwave but didn't turn it on. Instead, she pushed the button on the under counter radio and slid in a CD. She needed to be in his arms.

He complied, wrapping his strong ones around her and twirling her. Her kitchen wasn't all that big, so they pushed back the table and two chairs, and danced.

They both kicked off their shoes so their stockinged feet slid across the tile silently. He pulled her closer and she felt the shape of her body soften into his. She melted, willingly.

When the song ended, they both felt the desire. Rob, bless his heart, said, "What about those Nachos?"

~

They had both forgotten about taking down the tree in the shop. Maybe, they decided, it could wait a day, and Noelle and Braydon would help. Her mother used to leave the family tree up until February. Rob finally rose to leave and kissed her on her nose.

Cindy closed the door behind him. And wept.

She wiped her tears with a paper towel. Its rough surface hurt her eyes. Why was this happening? The first and only man she felt such a connection with; the only one she felt love for? No, she couldn't do it. What was God thinking? She wasn't strong enough.

Phone ringing. Candy. "You okay, girl? What happened?"

She shared. "Not strong." That's all she said.

"I am coming over. Now. Let me in."

~

Candy found Cindy crumpled in a heap in the corner of her sofa. She was holding a huge wad of tissues, and her head hung so low it almost disappeared between her shoulders.

"Cindy?"

"Hi," was the whispered response. She still didn't look up.

"Look at me," Candy commanded as she tried to lift Cindy's chin. Cindy shrugged her off.

"Go away. Please." Her voice was barely a whimper.

"Not on your life, girl. We are going to talk."

"Don't wanna."

"Tough. Do you need an intervention? Maybe I should call all the others."

"NO! This is private." Cindy jerked upright and shook her head vigorously. "You – okay. You understand."

"Look," Candy said. "What concerns one of us, concerns all of us. I know in my heart the other Candy Canes would understand."

"Yeh. Give advice, or worse, sympathy." Cindy shook her head again.

At least she's reacting, Candy thought. *That's progress.* She shimmied in beside her and grabbed the hand Cindy tried to pull away. "I will not let go. I will not go away." She reached for Cindy's other hand and turned her toward her. "Now talk!"

Cindy stared off in the distance, then tilted her head like she was searching for God in the ceiling. "Why me?"

"Why not you?" Candy said. "Why Dev? Why Rob?" She squeezed Cindy's fingers. "We are all God's children; we all have weaknesses, and, if we use them, we all have strengths." She smiled wanly. "God is an equal opportunity God."

~

Rob felt rotten. Why had he led Cindy on? Dancing, yet. What had he expected of her? It wasn't as if they had claimed undying love for each other. They were barely dating. Most of their contact had been working in Braydon's flower shop. Of course, being in his and Noelle's wedding.

It had all started with dancing, something they both loved to do, and an excuse to be close. Too close? Not for him, but he noticed she trembled when he drew her body close, especially since he had made the AA confession to her. And … he still hadn't made the other confession. Too much to overload her with. Was he right?

Do no harm. That really isn't exactly a step in the AA program, but Rob felt as if it should be. Did he harm Cindy by leading her on? Or, expecting too much of her?

Should he call? He prayed about it, and he pushed the Cindy button. If only she will pick up this late.

~

Cindy struggled with the covers. She groped on her nightstand. Something was buzzing. Her alarm didn't buzz, it chimed. Her fingers found the slightly moving, vibrating thing. Her phone! It was almost midnight. Who would call this late? Did Candy reveal her problems to the other Candy Canes? No, she trusted Candy. She had promised. Candy Canes always kept their promises.

Wiping the sleep from her eyes, she looked at the screen on the phone. Agh, Rob. Hadn't he done enough damage? Was he stalking her? Should she answer? Should she be scared? Of Rob?

Waking up a bit more, she realized that was a silly notion. Nothing about Rob was scary to her personally. Everything about Rob and his situation was scary ... to her personally. IF there was to be any future for them. She wished he had kept his secret to himself. But, that would have been deceptive, and Rob was not a dishonest person. He was an honest, upfront man.

She picked up the phone.

"Hi. Why are you calling?" That sounded lame, but it was the middle of the night.

Silence. Then a snuffle. From Rob?

She heard him suck in his breath, clear his throat, then croak out some words. "I am a fool."

"What?" She held the phone away and pushed speaker. "What are you saying, Rob? And, why now in the middle of the night?"

"Saying sorry. Sorry for leading you on." He was still croaking, or was he choking? Cindy wasn't sure, but his voice was filled with emotion. "When I realized I was falling in love with you," big pause, more sucked in breath, "I should have ended our relationship."

"What did you say? Please repeat the falling in love part." She knew she was teasing him, especially when he was so serious. Maybe it would lift him out of his doldrums. Surely, he didn't really mean the falling in love part. Did he?

"Not funny, Cindy. True."

"Oh, Rob, I feel the same way" she admitted.

"That's why I am so scared." She blinked her eyes to hold back the tears. This man was too much. This man is special, but she, Strong Cindy, leader of the Candy Canes, felt weak.

"I am weak. You are strong. Or," she said, "did Jesus say the opposite? Bible verses were never my forte, not remembering them anyway."

"I think He said that we are weak. He is the strong one. For us. He carries our burdens."

The tears finally escaped and trailed down Cindy's cheeks. Good thing sheets were so handy for wiping. She mumbled her great grandma Roberta's famous saying, "It will all work out."

"Mmm. I suppose. See you tomorrow at the shop to take down the Christmas tree with Noelle and Braydon?"

"Nine-thirty." She smacked a kiss and this time turned off her phone.

CHAPTER TEN

*T*he doors to Love In Joy Floral were wide open when Cindy arrived. She heard laughter. Such a good sign. She tried to slip in quietly, but Noelle caught her.

"Hey, girl! So good to see you."

"You, too, Madam Bride. How was Hawaii?" Cindy didn't want to ask how the honeymoon was. That was private. But, she hoped.

Before Noelle could answer, Braydon hugged her in a major squeeze. "How's my favorite sister-in-law, and thanks for coping with the shop while we … " He paused. Noelle bumped him on the arm and grinned. "While we had fun."

"You both sound and look so happy. And tanned." Cindy felt it was a lame comment, but it covered the situation. Both Noelle and Braydon grinned and winked to each other. Must be special to be so in love.

Rob came up and touched her arm. She smiled at him, hopefully warmly. "Hi, Rob." Keep it simple, Cindy. He nodded and squeezed her arm where his hand still lingered. Was there moisture in his eyes?

"Time for girl catchup," Noelle announced. "Love my guy, but miss my Candy Canes." She grabbed Cindy's hand and pulled her behind the arch into the back room.

When they were both seated at the little table where breaks were taken with donuts and coffee and where Braydon would do his paperwork, Cindy realized Noelle was sitting facing her.

"Well?" That was all Noelle said.

"What do you mean? Did Candy call you?" Cindy realized she had said too much. Needed to learn to keep her mouth shut.

"No. What do *you* mean? Why would Candy call me ... on my honeymoon?" Noelle leaned across the table and looked Cindy straight in the eyes. "Well?"

"It's just that, it's just that ..." Cindy repeated. "I needed advice. She gave it. End of story."

"Really? I don't think so, not from your reluctance to share." Noelle grabbed one of Cindy's retreating hands and wouldn't let go. "Now, tell me." It was a command.

Cindy shared, reluctantly. But, this was Noelle who married Rob's brother. She stumbled over the words, but finally got them out. "I am scared. To death. But, I love him."

Noelle pushed back her chair and rushed around the table to hug Cindy in a strong embrace. Cindy collapsed in her arms. "Hey," Noelle said, "What are Candy Canes for?"

"This," she heard Cindy mumble.

~

"I am worried about Cindy ... and Rob." Noelle

snuggled next to Braydon, still in awe that he is now her husband. She poked her nose into his neck and ran her fingers through the wiry, curly hairs on his chest. How did it happen? How had she become so blessed?

Braydon turned toward her. "They are both adults. Both Christians. What's to worry?"

Noelle sat up in bed and yanked the covers. "How can you be so insensitive? To your brother, and the woman he obviously loves?"

Uh, oh. First fight. And, not about them, but about their siblings and dear friends. Well, Noelle thought of Cindy as a sister, always had. All of the Candy Canes were sisters – in swimming competition and in love for Jesus. They supported each other always. Remembering Doreen's accident was the crux.

Braydon turned over and pulled the covers up. "Go to sleep, Noelle. God will take care of it."

~

Cindy felt helpless. And angry. She wasn't sure if she was mad at Rob for not telling her sooner about his condition, as she called it, or at herself for her lack of empathy. Even more so for falling in love with him. She was so upset she whispered words she never used, spitting them out of her lips to form steam in the unusually cold weather. Maybe she should take up drinking. That would show him!

What convoluted thinking. She had to talk with someone, someone who could give her insight, and hopefully peace. She thought of that old hymn they used to sing in her parents' traditional church about peace in my soul, peace like a river. She attended a contemporary evangelical church – no traditional hymns. Sometimes the old ones were so soothing.

Yes, she needed to talk with someone who could give her more understanding. She thought first of Braydon, but that might seem as if she was undermining Noelle. She knew Noelle and Candy were sincere and loving friends, but she needed understanding from someone close to Rob, maybe someone who had made the journey with him. She didn't know any of the other AA members personally, although she guessed she had met a few on Christmas Eve at the Lovejoys. Suddenly it hit her. She clapped her hands and mouthed "Thank you, Lord." But, was she brave enough to call, and would her fears and concerns be accepted?

~

Lydia Lovejoy opened the door and opened her arms. She led Cindy into her kitchen and set a cup of steaming coffee in front of her on the antique wooden table. "Sugar? Cream or flavored creamer?" she asked. "Or would you prefer tea? I just assumed." A little chuckle escaped her mouth as she pulled out a chair across the table from Cindy.

Cindy shook her head to all the beverage questions and wrapped her hands around the warm mug. Where to begin? She needn't have worried. Rob's mother spoke first.

"I think I know why you're here." She smiled reassuringly, a smile that put Cindy at ease, even though she continued to stare into the brown liquid in her cup. "I'm glad you came. Hopefully I can reassure you and, as women, we can bolster each other up." Lydia cocked her head to one side and seemed to be searching Cindy's face.

"Mrs. Lovejoy, I don't know where to begin. Or,

even how."

"First of all, please remember you agreed to call me Lydia. Now, begin at the beginning." She fiddled with the handle of her own mug, then tapped dainty fingernails on the table. "You're in love with him." It was a statement, not a question.

Cindy felt heat creeping up her neck. She nodded. "Of course you would guess. Why else would I come to you?"

"Oh, maybe to ask where I found this antique table, or the funky mismatched chairs," she quipped. She reached across the table to touch one of Cindy's hands. "I'm glad he has fallen in love, and," she continued, "with you."

"Really? Why me?"

"Because you are a sincere, Christian girl, and a strong one according to Rob. I also know you are clever and creative from the signs you made for the shop. I also know you must love children. I know not all preschool teachers do; some teach just for a job; mostly those who don't have a four year college education. But, I know enough about New Hope to know how conscientious your director is in hiring. She and the school have a stellar reputation." She stopped there. "Whew. I think I just gave an advertisement for the preschool, and for the woman my son loves."

Cindy dabbed at her eyes with the paper napkin in front of her. This woman would make a wonderful mother-in-law. Lucky Noelle.

Suddenly she realized what Lydia had said. "… the woman my son loves."

"H … how do you know? That he loves me, I mean." She felt like a fool, but she had to ask.

"It's obvious," Lydia said. "Besides he told me last night when he came to ask for my advice." Was that a smug grin on the older woman's face?

"Oh. He came here?" Was he a mama's boy?

"Yes. He and Braydon still share with their old mom. Their dad, too." She nodded, and the grin appeared again. "Logan is a wonderful father, but there's nothing like a mother's advice, even for a grown man."

Cindy wished she had a mom. Why did hers commit suicide ten years ago? As a Christian, that broke her heart doubly. Especially since Mom had professed faith. Would that profession of faith allow her to enter heaven? She blinked back more tears. This mind wandering wasn't getting her anywhere. "Could you, would you be willing, to share Rob's story with me? I need to understand – a lot more than I do."

~

Cindy leaned back against the headrest. She had stuck the key in the ignition, but couldn't make herself turn it. So many words and images zoomed through her mind. Especially the statement Lydia had said. "…the woman my son loves." That was a biggie. Yes, Rob had told her on the phone he loves her, but to share with his mother … wow!

Lydia had described in detail about his arrest. She could almost see the police cars out in front of the Lovejoy home, the ones that had followed him from his attempted drug sale. She envisioned Lydia praying in the corner of her front porch, her secret room she'd said, like Jesus said in the Bible in Matthew. It was all so unbelievable. Yet, Lydia swore Rob had given her permission to share. That was over five years ago, at least. Her mind was swimming with so much information. Swimming! Such a perfect analogy for a Candy Cane. Now, she had to decide. What stroke should she use in her relationship with Rob? She was tempted to do backstroke, but that seemed cowardly, and it was Doreen's official stroke, the one she won competition with as the anchor.

Cindy was the best freestyler on the team. That's why she always led, to set the pace for the others. But, what did that mean in life? How did it transfer?

Just before she turned on the ignition she remembered Rob's mom's last remark. "Did he mention anything else?" She had blinked her eyes several times and sort of mumbled. "Never mind. His call." Then a friendly, warm, "Goodbye, dear. Call me any time."

What was "anything else?" More secrets?

She thumped her hands on the steering wheel, gripped it hard, and drove home.

CHAPTER ELEVEN

Rob banged around, slamming his fists into walls and tables and overturning chairs. He knew Cindy was meeting with his mom, Mom told him. Just like her. He wished he hadn't known. So much easier. Finally, he poured a cup of really strong coffee and called his mom.

"Robinson, stop! Stop this worrying. Stop!"

"Mom, it's hard. I have never felt this way about a woman before. Do you know she stepped on my toes?"

Silence. Then, "What on earth are you talking about?"

"At the wedding. We were dancing, and Cindy stepped on my toes, just as we started to twirl."

"Fond memory, I hope." Lydia paused before going on. "So? Does that mean she is a no or a yes?" He could almost see the expression of confusion on her face. Mom was so transparent, even over the phone.

Without warning, Dad grabbed the phone. He was always no nonsense, right to the point. "Do you love her?"

Rob nodded, then realized they couldn't hear the rattling in his head. "Yes."

"Does she love you?" his dad said.

"I think so. Ask Mom who spent some time with her today."

This time he could almost hear Mom's head rattling. Dad came back on. "Then, go for it, son! Don't waste time. God sometimes gives us one opportunity to make things right. This may be yours."

~

Lydia's words came back to Cindy. "I felt as if Rob was a stranger. How could I have not seen the signs? Some of them weren't even subtle."

Cindy felt the same way. Surely she would have seen signs in Rob's demeanor and behavior. Yet, he always seemed so normal, so sincere, so above board. Always the gentleman, and the best dancer in history. She grinned to herself. Was that what attracted her to him?

She reminded herself, however, that he was five years sober. Of course she wouldn't see any obvious signs. Candy did tell her that often even recovering alcoholics still have some behaviors that linger – mostly personality behaviors. She was sure he didn't sneak an occasional drink, or even act like he wanted one. He did have a stubborn streak, didn't like anyone to tell him what to do, or how. She was sort of like that, too, she realized – team leader type. Well, she had a strong personality. After all, she was used to corralling dozens of three and four year olds, but in a sweet voice and diplomatic manner. Yet, there were times when she blew it and had to be very firm.

She laughed to herself remembering little Justin's comment right before Christmas break. The kids were so excited, chattering about Santa and reindeer and the toys they had asked him for. Of course as soon as she had lined them up for the Christmas pageant, at least three of them had to go to the bathroom. To make potty time more difficult, the little girls were all dressed as angels in long white gowns made from sheets, and the boys were shepherds attired in brown burlap cotton sacks with oversized cotton headbands. Thank goodness her wonderful co-teacher, Mandy, offered to take them. She knew Mandy would do the deed as quickly as possible, but would the kids? It was especially hard with the girls because their angel wings got in the way of holding up their skirts. Finally, she heard the toilets between the shared classrooms flush three times just as she heard Miss Patti the music minister call for her class. Mandy led the children back to their places, but she was holding a big wad of paper towels on little Tiffany's wings soaking up wetness.

Cindy had thanked Mandy, rolled her eyes and firmly said, "Children, your parents and families are waiting for you to sing your beautiful songs. Everybody ready now?"

Apparently, her voice had an edge to it; something she tried to not happen. But, it must have, for four year old Justin made a loud announcement. "Miss Cindy mad. You guys all behave."

Yes, she probably had been mad, more at herself than the children. She should have insisted each child go potty before donning their costumes. All her fault.

She rolled over in bed trying to put her conversation with Lydia Lovejoy in perspective. She was sure Lydia liked her; she was even almost sure the woman hoped she would be her daughter-in-law. Someday. What she wasn't sure of was how she felt. She finally fell asleep seeking the Lord's guidance. She was too tired to figure it out.

~

The dratted phone was buzzing again. Hopefully Rob doing one of his pre-midnight calls.
She was tempted to ignore it. Was calling this late one of the latent signs of his disease? One of
the lingering signs? Maybe he had trouble sleeping and calling her helped him calm down.

She reached for the phone vibrating on her nightstand. "Hi. You okay?"

The voice on the other end was female, and nasty. "I am *not* okay," it said. "You stole him from me."

Cindy rubbed the sleep from her eyes. Who was this person? "Who," she finally managed to ask, "are you?"

She knew her words were slurred from sleep, but she had to know. Was this an old flame of Rob's? Had he professed love to her as he had to Cindy?

"Doesn't matter who I am. For five years we have supported each other, said we loved each other, too." The person on the other end sucked in a deep breath. "He is mine. Always will be. So buzz off. Leave him alone."

Cindy heard a click. The other woman was gone, and she lay in her bed still clutching her phone.

CHAPTER TWELVE

She needed to do something active, something to work off worry and frustration. The holiday break was almost over, and Cindy knew from the way her jeans fit she had gained some inches. She could always go to Natalie's gym, but machines and free weights didn't sound appealing. Swimming did. The community Candy's parents lived in had two pools. She was sure they would lend her a key.

She rooted around in her bottom dresser drawer, the depository for seldom used items. The bikini was a no. She felt too chunky for it, plus it wasn't all that comfortable for actual swimming – more like for sunning on the beach. Wadded in the corner was her old red and white striped team suit, the one she had worn as part of the Candy Canes. It would have to do, if only she could still fit into it. Even if it was tight, it would cover most of her body. With a few groans and tugs she pulled it on, then she called Candy's parents.

Mrs. Ashford answered on the first ring. After a

brief conversation during which the dear lady exclaimed, "How delightful to hear your voice, Cynthia!" she said, "Of course you may borrow our key. I'm excited another Candy Cane will be working out there."

Cindy attempted to explain she wasn't "working out" for any competition, just to hopefully lose some holiday excess. Why had she imbibed in chocolate so much? And of all things, candy canes and Jelly Bellies? Probably she had made the excuse she craved them and had no reason not to. Now, with the possibility of Rob in her life, she did have a reason. Surely, he wasn't attracted to fat women.

She wondered about the female voice on the phone, the threatening one who refused to give her name. Had Rob been more to her than a friend? Was she in AA with Rob? Or, an old flame? Probably in AA since the strident voice claimed his love and support for five years, and both Rob and his mother said he'd joined AA five years ago. Could she compete with someone he'd been close to for five years? But, how close? Was it mutual, or did the woman embellish their relationship?

On her way to pick up the pool key from Mrs. Ashford she thought how nice it would be to have companionship. All the articles she'd read about working out and losing weight suggested having a buddy, someone to keep you on track, to keep tabs. She wasn't sure how or why she thought about Melanie. Maybe God put the new member of the Candy Canes on her heart. Maybe she needed a friend, too.

At the stoplight Cindy searched for Melanie's phone number. Only a busy signal, no voice mail to leave a message. Feeling a bit like a Johnny Come Lately, she flung the phone on the passenger seat of her car.

She was turning into the first entrance off San Miguel Boulevard to Harbor View Homes when her phone buzzed. What? Rob's name came up. Not what she had expected. Should she answer? She pulled over on a side street named Port Cardigan. As always when she visited this community, she wondered why all the streets, except one, were named Port streets. They were almost two miles from the Pacific, and certainly not near any port. In fact, she couldn't think of any actual port in Newport Beach. Maybe years ago?

She stopped her car and pulled over in front of an obviously remodeled house, large and opulent with an original one-story plain stucco on either side. "Hang on," she mouthed while parking. "Okay. What?" Silence on the other end. Had he hung up?

"I guess I deserved that."

"Well, maybe. Since your old girlfriend called me, and," she added, "threatened me."

"What? Who?"

"I have no idea because she refused to give her name. But, she was angry and nasty and very confrontational." Cindy bit her lip. "Can you imagine how I felt?"

"What did she say … specifically?"

"Mostly that you and she had supported each other for five years." Cindy decided to reveal the most important part of the other woman's conversation, if one could call it that since there had been minimal exchange. "I assumed she was from your AA group, but she didn't say. She did say you told her you loved her, and I was to butt out. Leave you alone. "

Nothing but silence on Rob's end. Cindy almost pushed the red button on her phone. Did he really have to think about this?

"Cindy, would you be willing to come to an AA meeting with me? So, you can see what takes place?"

"Maybe. Yes, okay. When? Not tonight."

"Tomorrow after church? Noon? Last day before end of Christmas break."

"Okay. Give me directions." Then she added, "Do I get to meet this woman?"

She heard another call coming in. "Gotta go. Text directions to me. K?"

Melanie was calling her back. She had seen Cindy's number on her cell. Yes, she would love to meet her at the pool and swim laps. Good competition for both. And companionship. Much needed.

~

She almost didn't recognize her. Her long hair was cut in a bob. Super cute Cindy thought, then remembered to tell her so. Melanie was not as trim in stature as most of the Candy Canes, but Cindy didn't think she was either, lately. They slapped palms and dove in.

After ten laps they both collapsed on the chaise lounge chairs around the pool.

"Whew, that was quite a workout." Melanie said in a gasping voice.

"Yep." Cindy was grateful she still had breath.

"You gals must have been great. I can't even imagine."

"In high school we practiced every day, sometimes for hours. Gave us an edge. Coach Douglas always asked for extra practice time. I think he got it because Vista Del Mar wanted so much to have a winning state team. And," she added, "we did!"

"Three years in a row? And it started when you were all only sophomores?"

Cindy saw Melanie's eyes widen. "Yes, we were very blessed." Then, she added, "Did you know we were all Christians? Still are?"

"So, you prayed together? Did that help?"

"Made all the difference. We had, and still do have, a deep faith. We stick together with God."

Cindy grabbed a towel she'd brought and started to dry her hair. Squeezing out the moisture in her long tresses she noticed Melanie was staring off in space.

"You okay?" she asked.

"What? Yes. I guess."

"You hesitated."

"I know. It's just that … that …." Melanie closed her eyes. Cindy wondered if from the bright sun or if she was in thought. She leaned over and touched Melanie's hand.

"Something is bothering you. Wanna share?"

"It's not important." Melanie wavered again. "Really."

"Well," Cindy said, "if you change your mind, I'm a good listener." The heat of the sun made her drowsy. She wrapped the towel around her head, pushed her sunglasses up high on her nose and reclined on the chaise. Just as she started to drift off, Melanie spoke.

"I do."

"You do what?"

"Want to share." Her face was ashen when she turned toward Cindy.

~

Her words drifted in the air like dirty snowflakes seeking a mud puddle.

Cindy barely understood a word Melanie said, but she caught a few between incoherent mumblings. "Crazy, drugged, lost baby, hate. Guilty, so guilty."

Cindy's heart broke for Melanie.

Loss of purity! But, more than that. Drugs, promiscuity, loss of self.

Melanie poured her heart out to Cindy. Guilt almost drowned her.

"When my dad died, I was so angry, so bitter." Melanie paused to let the tears fall, then turned toward Cindy again. "I went ballistic, out of control." She shook her head as if to shake off the memories. "I suddenly had a new group of friends. Don't know why, except they sensed my fear and loneliness and unworthiness." She shook her head again. "They became my anchor."

Cindy didn't know what to say, had so many questions to ask. But, instead, she just hugged. She wiped the other girl's tears with her towel.

Yes, Melanie did need to be led to Jesus, but was Cindy the one to do it? She found some Bible verses on her cell phone about forgiveness and Christ never leaving believers. But, Melanie needed more than random verses, especially since she wasn't grounded in the Bible. Cindy even wondered about how grounded she herself was. Because of work, she seldom got to attend Bible study. She had even skipped church twice over Christmas break. And, instead of going to the Christmas Eve service as she'd planned, she was at the Lovejoys with Rob. If she could call it "being with"

Rob. Mostly she was with the Candy Canes and some of Rob's surfing buddies and a few female friends of his who she now was sure were also AA. That must have been the tap on the shoulder one girl gave to another across the back of Cindy's chair. Not wanting to give Rob away.

Mariners Church where she attended did have a Thursday evening Bible study. Not only was she tired after a long day with three year olds, but Fridays were usually the days the children's parents came early to the classroom to collect the crafts they had made during the week. So, Cindy spent extra time cleaning up the room and scraping paste off the tables. Still, she needed to make a special effort for Melanie. She also believed the hurting woman needed to form friendships with other believers. Especially older ones who could mentor her. Maybe some who had been through what she had. One of her favorite authors Mark Batterson quotes his grandma as saying, "You never, ever, sometimes never know." Or something like that. She grinned to herself.

Maybe Lydia Lovejoy would have an idea. She wouldn't reveal Melanie's secret, but she could explain a friend who believes she had committed a great sin and wants to know Jesus needs a Christian women's group. She felt close to the woman now that they had had their own little talk, so she was comfortable calling her. Or, she could call Noelle's mom Kerstin. She, too, had a deep faith, but she was very involved in her gardening club. Still, Cindy didn't know what else she was a part of. She remembered the story Noelle told about how Braydon gave a presentation at the Harbor View Garden Club, and Kerstin won a rose bush Noelle helped Braydon plant.

Cindy was about to give up and leave a message when Lydia answered. The two women laughed about how long it takes to get from the bathroom to the phone. Lydia was understanding and didn't ask questions, except, "Does she have a church home?"

Cindy wasn't sure, but she did sort of invite Melanie to attend the ten o'clock service at Mariners next weekend. She doubted Melanie had much Christian upbringing or she would at least have mentioned a church she attended, if only occasionally.

"Let's get started with that," Lydia said. "Mariners is a Bible teaching church, but it is big. I hope that won't intimidate her. Some people are more comfortable with smaller, more intimate places of worship. Or," she pondered, "she might feel better being lost in a crowd."

Before they hung up, Lydia asked in a hesitant voice, "Has Rob called you lately?" Cindy assured her he had. She did sense more of a question than the one Lydia offered. Again she wondered if there was another secret.

She decided to call Kerstin next. A just in case, backup call. Noelle's mother was enthusiastic about helping Melanie, even though Cindy never revealed her name, just said she is a Candy Cane. The only thing that disturbed her was Kerstin asking, "Are you all right? You sure it's not personal, about you? I can keep a secret. Honest."

Oh, dear. Although she never revealed Melanie's secret sin, she implied it was pretty devastating. Did Kerstin, maybe even Lydia, think she was asking for help for herself? Surely, both knew she was strong in her faith. Or, did they?

She hoped the two mothers of special friends, especially Rob's mom Lydia, did not think she was confessing and needing help and support. She could always use both, but not for the reason she had shared. What had she gotten herself into?

~

Rob called. This time at about eight. "What did you do today? Something fun and relaxing on one of the last days of break?"

Cindy wondered, was even a little taken back, by his question. Had he spoken with his mom?

"I had a great time swimming and working off some calories. You?"

"I went to a realtors' meeting. Not an AA one, a business one."

"Was it good?"

"Sort of." He paused. "It was the old blah, blah, blah about how to increase business, what to put on websites, etc." Then, he said, "I knew it all. It was just repeat."

"Oh, sorry it wasn't more informative."

"S'okay. I just needed to appear. Part of the deal." Cindy realized too much silence on his end. Maybe a two minute break?

"I wish I had known, would have prayed for you."

"Really? You would have. For a meeting?"

"Sure. Everything, every experience is worth praying about."

CHAPTER THIRTEEN

She agreed to go with Rob in his car to the meeting. Silly to waste gas, and she was still a bit leery about how reliable her car was. They pulled up to a small church, its parking lot filled with cars of all types. While she was gathering her enormous purse, Rob came around to open the door for her. "Such a gentleman. Thanks."

Just as he made an elaborate bow and took her hand, they heard a strident high-pitched voice behind him. "Is this *her*?" The woman behind Rob was tall and lanky, almost as tall as Rob. Her face was pasty and her lips curled in anger. But, Cindy noticed, she had long luxurious blond hair she had flung over one shoulder, like the woman who had sat next to her on Christmas Eve at the Lovejoy's. If it weren't for the ugly expression on her face, she would be stunning.

Rob spun around leaving Cindy standing at the open car door. She could tell from his voice he was trying to be civil, but the set of his shoulders and the way he had abruptly dropped her hand, told her it took him a lot of control. "Emily." His voice sounded surprised, or at least he tried to make it sound that way. "I'd like you to meet my friend, Cindy."

Emily sneered and made no move to step forward. Cindy felt as if the other woman was mentally undressing her. Still, she graciously held her hand out and smiled. Her hand hovered in mid-air, but she kept the smile pasted on her face. She was almost positive Emily was the nasty voice on the phone. But, how did she get Cindy's number? Question for Rob, later.

Rob turned back to Cindy, and in a noble gesture held out an elbow to each woman. "Let's go in. Shall we?"

Cindy tucked her right hand in the crook of his arm and squeezed lightly. "Thank you, Mr. Gentleman." Emily ignored his arm and scowled. Still, she trotted beside him with clipped steps in spike-heeled red patent shoes.

Rob led Cindy to an empty chair close to his surfing buddies, probably to make her more comfortable since she'd already met them. He took a single chair up front after confirming with her he had seated her all right. Nick and Brad both acknowledged her with smiles and winks. Finally, Brad said, "You AA, too?"

Cindy knew he was curious. Why did she feel offended by his question? She wasn't embarrassed to be with Rob, nor to be sitting with them. She shook her head. "No, just a guest. If Rob and I are going to be part of each other's lives, he wants me to understand."

Nick leaned across Brad and stage whispered, "Great idea." He hesitated, probably screwing up his courage. "You, Cindy," pause, "it is Cindy, isn't it?" She nodded and smiled. What a nice man, what a nice friend for Rob to have. "You, Cindy," he repeated, "are the best thing to happen to Rob in the twelve years I've known him."

Cindy was … what was that word her grandmother used to use? Flabbergasted. What a nice compliment, so encouraging.

Nick must have felt his comment necessary to explain. "We started surfing together when we were about eighteen. That lazy summer after high school before college hit us. We also started partying a lot." Cindy noticed his eyes glazed a bit before he continued. "If it weren't for Rob, I wouldn't be here." He stopped to look into her face, and she felt her cheeks heat with color. "He is such an encourager, and such an example."

She was about to acknowledge his comments when she heard Rob's clear voice. "My name is Rob, and I am an alcoholic." He was standing up front behind a small wooden podium, although he wasn't gripping it as many people would for security. His arms hung comfortably at his sides. His eyes seemed to scan the group of almost thirty people there on the folding chairs. Finally, his gaze locked on Cindy's face. "Before I tell you my story, I want to introduce you to my guest, Cindy." He gestured toward her, and Brad sitting beside her held her arm up. Cindy grinned, but felt the color creeping into her face again.

"Cindy," Rob went on, "is not an alcoholic. She is blessed to take a glass of wine with the wonderful Nachos she creates." A few giggles. "Because she is special," he went on, "because I love her and hope to make her my wife ... well, that's why she's here." Now, Rob was blushing, and the AA audience was clapping wildly. "I haven't officially asked her yet, though." He stopped again looking right at her. "Cindy, I know this isn't the most romantic proposal, and I am planning on getting down on one knee. But, it seemed right to me."

Cindy's eyes filled with tears that spilled down her face, and she was sure, very rosy cheeks. Brad pulled her up, supporting her with a strong arm and forcing her to stand on wobbly legs. She nodded. Wow, what a dramatic proposal. Rob must have seen how protective Brad was, and how Nick had stepped in front of her to support her emotionally and physically on her other side. Rob seemed to glow. She noticed Emily, who had sat near the front also, got up to leave. As the woman started awkwardly climbing over several others' feet, Rob stopped her with words.

"Emily. Please don't leave. Your turn is next. Oh, well, you can hear my personal story next time." And he stepped away from the wobbly podium. But, in true Rob fashion, he held out his hand to lead her to the front. She grasped it, jerked at her blouse to straighten it, and with Rob's guidance took her turn. Hands clasped tightly in front of her, she stammered. "Hi. I'm Emily, and I am an alcoholic." Everyone clapped.

Cindy closed her eyes and prayed for her, for courage and understanding. Finally, after a loud breath, Emily said, "This is an unusual meeting. I owe Rob an apology, and," she hesitated a long time, "Cindy, too.

"That," she said, "is all I can say tonight. Except, thank you all for being here. Please fellowship after the meeting. Coffee is in the back."

~

Cindy leaned across the car console against Rob's shoulder. "Life is complicated," she finally whispered. She wasn't exactly sure how she felt, a combination of thrilled and excited, and embarrassed and sad. What a strange afternoon.

"Yes, it can be if we let it."

"But?"

"If we trust in the Lord to work all things for good … well, as my Grandma Robbie used to say, 'It will all work out.'"

And, it did.

~

Rob started to follow her into her condo. He felt there was so much left unsaid after his public proposal during the meeting. This time he wanted to do it right. But, Cindy stopped him with an upheld hand.

"No. Not tonight. Need to sort things out. Sorry." She kissed him on his cheek and inserted her key in the door.

When the door closed firmly and he heard the security lock click, he turned away. He couldn't figure out why, but his first thought was for Emily. How could that be when he loved Cindy so much?

He knew that even though never intended, he felt sorry for Emily and owed her an explanation. She had misunderstood his gestures of friendship and support. A lot of AA people hugged and told others they loved them, because they did, as friends and supporters and fellow members. Emily had obviously taken it wrong. Too wrong.

He knocked on her door. He had been there once before, but not romantically. She had been very unstable, very worried how she could go through the program and not backslide. Although Rob wasn't her sponsor, he'd decided to help. Maybe that was his mistake; maybe he should have stepped back and let her sponsor take over.

He heard her approach the door, and he prayed for guidance.

~

Cindy answered his phone call and agreed he could come over, especially since he had something to tell her. What, she wondered? She was still overwhelmed from his public display of affection and proposal.

She opened her door and gasped. Trying to avoid looking at the two people standing on her stoop, she lifted her eyes above them and saw a shooting star. She'd never seen one before. Was it a sign? Lowering her gaze to the faces in front of her, she simply said, "Hello." Was that rude? She didn't care. What was Rob doing here with Emily clinging to his arm? Why were her lips quivering and a tear sliding down one cheek making a little track in her makeup? How bizarre they should be here, together.

Rob lowered his head. "May we come in … please?"

Cindy opened the door wider and felt her heart pound fitfully. Her hand was still on the doorknob, but she couldn't move it. Rob pushed past her practically dragging Emily.

~

Cindy collapsed on the sofa clutching a wad of tissue. She hadn't even bothered to get up to close the door behind them. She was in a stupor. It was still difficult to breathe. Finally, she leaned forward resting her elbows on her knees and her forehead in her hands. Her turn to sob. She wasn't sure if for the other woman, herself, or Rob, or them all. Besides Emily's embarrassment and confessing her torch for Rob, "I misunderstood his kindness. His hugs led me to believe, no, want to believe, he cared for me romantically." She had turned first to Rob, then hesitantly to Cindy. "My fault. Sorry," she mumbled.

Cindy remembered nodding. That was all. Just nodding. She thought about the shooting star. Why had the only time she'd seen one happened just then? Was it a wakeup call from God? She would probably never know, but she knew she would never forget the moment.

Rob had his arm across Emily's shoulder when they stumbled out the door. Yes, he is a kind man, always caring about others. He had turned slightly and spoke firmly. "I'm coming back."

Did she want him to? It would be awkward.

~

Rob was glad he had gone to Emily's and taken her to Cindy's. He did feel sorry for the poor girl. Hopefully, made it clear he cared about her as a person and fellow AA member, but he was not in love with her, only Cindy. They had talked about the AA steps, and Emily had finally said, "Need to make amends." She had looked at him pleadingly. "Can you take me to her? I'm scared to go alone. I'm sure she'd slam the door in my face."

Rob doubted that. Cindy was sensitive and kind. But, knowing Emily was ashamed, he gave in and drove her there. Stupid! He should have had her follow in her car. Now, he had to take her home. He hadn't been thinking beyond the moment. Neither spoke on the way back to Emily's apartment. He dropped her off and watched while she unlocked her door. Both waved, and he pulled away wondering what he would find when he got to Cindy's. He pushed the button to open the center console in his Mercedes and felt around until his fingers touched velvet. Laughing to himself, he was pretty sure Cindy had a sense of humor. Would she get it? Would she understand the fake diamond, really a chunk of glass in a tacky band, was not an offense? He wanted her to go with him to choose her own ring, one she would love to wear for all time. But, he also wanted a symbol of love for when he officially proposed.

His hand holding the tiny box shook a little as he pushed the doorbell. The moment of truth was about to come.

~

Cindy walked slowly to the door. Her legs felt like wooden posts. She knew it would be Rob, and she prayed he wasn't playing a game. Or worse, coming to break up with her.

"Lovely lady." His voice was deep, but it trembled a little. "Please sit on the couch."

She did, back straight and legs demurely crossed at her ankles. She felt her lips quiver when she tried to smile. Rob took her left hand in his two large ones and knelt on the carpet in front of her. Before he did, though, he had to push the coffee table back to make room for his large frame. Then, when his knee made a popping sound, she almost lost it.

"Ouch! Never done this before. Maybe I should have practiced." His throaty laugh made her laugh, too.

"I hope you haven't. Maybe you should have taken

lessons from your brother. You could have borrowed his Santa suit." Although Rob hadn't been present when Braydon proposed to Noelle, she was sure he could imagine. She remembered and was overcome with a spate of giggles. Had she spoiled the moment?

"Old surfing injury," he said as an explanation. "Let's try it this way." He rose to sit on the couch and wrapped one arm around her. Tilting her chin toward him, he leaned in to stroke her cheek and kiss her with so much passion his knee popped again. They both laughed. "Does that work?" he asked when he finally tore away from her lips to tickle her ear seductively with his tongue.

"Yes, Rob. It does." Cindy was breathless, but this time not from laughing. She took his strong jaws in her hands and pulled his face down to cling her lips to his in her own passionate kiss.

~

Rob almost skipped to his car. Although he had stammered and mumbled trying to explain about the fake ring, when it finally computed, she burst out laughing and hugged him so hard he wondered if his ribs would crack. Next Saturday they would go ring hunting.

CHAPTER FOURTEEN

*C*indy felt different, new. Was that what love does? She laid out her clothes for tomorrow, the end of break and first day of school. Navy slacks and a pale pink blouse. Pink wasn't usually a color she wore. In fact, this blouse still had the store tags on it. But, it was a love color, and she was definitely in love. Almost officially engaged. She couldn't wait to tell Dana and the other teachers. Even some parents she had gotten close to.

She decided to wear the imitation ring – for fun, and maybe a few laughs. Would anyone realize how phony it was? The stone was huge, set in a cheesy goldish band which gave it a sort of lop-sided look on her narrow finger. She couldn't wait to see the different reactions. One teacher, Myra, was married to a jeweler; or at least he worked at that fancy jewelry store in Balboa. She would probably spot it as a fake. Would she also give a fake congratulation? This could really be fun.

When she arrived at school in the morning and clocked in, she made a lot of gestures with her left hand. She asked Lorrie the office manager to sign her lesson plan by pushing the paper across her desk with her left hand. A dark cloud hovered over her. What had she expected? No angel wings flapped. Everyone was so busy getting their classrooms ready for the noisy onslaught of three and four and five year olds. Fortunately, being the organized person she was, she had set up her room before break. Now, she had nothing to do but wait.

Her cell rang. She forgot to turn it to mute. Melanie! Surely she must realize this was the first day back at school, and Cindy would be busy, even though she wasn't. She answered snappishly. "Hi. What?"

"Oh, sorry. Bad time?"

"First day of school. Waiting for students to arrive." She knew she was abrupt. "Sorry. What's up?"

"Not important. Never mind. Go back to your job." Click. She felt and heard the hurt in the other woman's squeaky voice. What kind of friend was she? Lousy.

She tried to call back, but the line buzzed busy. The alternative was to pray, so she did.

Her first student came in decked out in a Minion tee shirt. Little Alex puffed up his chest and pointed to the one-eyed character on the front of his shirt. Cindy bent down to his level and hugged him. Fortunately, hugs were still PC at this age. Just brief ones. His mom laughed as she handed him off with a "See you soon, bud." He seemed satisfied with that and plunked into his regular seat.

"What IS that, Ms. Cindy?" He was pointing to The Ring. "It's big."

CINDY'S PERFECT DANCE

Well, wouldn't you know a three year old would be the first to spy it? She tried to play it cool, be nonchalant. "Oh, Alex, you noticed. It's a ring."

"Can I see?" He reached across the small table and grasped her hand pulling it in front of him. "Yep. Big." Then he picked up a crayon and started to color.

~

The week seemed to speed by. Everyone was so busy making sure kids were comfortable and back on track. Ms. Dana had given several tours of the school for potential new parents and a few interviews for staff. Cindy knew the director always needed backups. One of the teachers was expecting a baby soon and would be taking off for at least several weeks, maybe months. The college age girl who helped with after care had joined a sorority and now had to attend meetings some afternoons.

Cindy walked into the office to clock out on Thursday. She was tired. Clean up today was challenging – so many bits of paper and gobs of glue on the tables. Mandy usually helped, but she was needed to answer phones since it was Lorrie's early day. As she walked past the reception desk, Mandy jerked her head toward the closed door of the director's office. Since there was no glass window, the door was solid, except for all the student drawings and parent comments scotch-taped to it.

"What?"

"Someone you know," was all Mandy said.

"Really? Who?"

"Not for me to say."

Then why had she brought it up? "Interview?"

Mandy nodded.

Cindy let it go. So, she knew someone, knew lots of people. Was none of her business. Time would tell, and so would Dana.

She clocked out, grabbed a cookie from the ever present tray of goodies and held her plastic key over the gate code. Just as she took a bite of the gooey chocolate confection and was readjusting her bag's shoulder strap she bumped into someone. Melanie!

Surprised to see each other, they hugged. "I tried to call you back, but line was busy. Then, I forgot. So sorry."

"It's okay. I wanted your recommendation, but guess I didn't need it." She grinned widely. "I'm in."

Cindy felt confused and probably showed it.

"I will be seeing you several afternoons a week. Not actually working with you, but near you." She beamed. "I will be helping with aftercare."

Cindy was almost overwhelmed. Could this be the same Melanie who had sobbed and confessed to her? "But, what about …?" Her question hung between them like drizzling rain on a sun-filled day.

"Oh, that. Your director does thorough background checks. I have never been arrested, Praise God. Just sinned." She looked at Cindy straight on. "God and I are taking care of that.

"And," she continued, "Pastor Steve is counseling me. Every Monday morning.

"I am forgiven."

Cindy's head spun. She had so many questions, but she would only pose one to Melanie. "What made you decide to apply to New Hope Preschool?"

"You, mostly. I love children and have always wanted to be a part of their lives. And," she offered, "as you might have guessed, I lost a child. I know that baby is in heaven, but," she lowered her eyes, "I want to be part of ensuring other children get there."

Cindy knew she looked puzzled. Melanie spoke again.

"No, I did not abort. Almost did, but I lost the baby at seventeen weeks. Stress the doctors called it. I do believe it was a he, a boy. His name is Jerimiah, Jerry for short. After the prophet."

They went out for coffee. Same table she and Rob had occupied in the corner. This time it wasn't a battlefield, but a field of dreams. Sort of like the movie, but not baseball. This dream field held personal hope for redemption of sin, and for the future. She was so proud of Melanie.

Cindy apologized for letting Melanie down about Sunday church. Melanie said she went anyway on her own and loved it. *Whew! Guess I am off the hook. Thank you, Lord. You always do provide.*

~

The call came close to midnight, again. She knew who to expect, so she answered with the "Hi, how are you?"

"Sorry, Cindy. It's me again, Emily."

"Heavens, Emily. I thought we were finished." Cindy sucked in a breath. "What's up? You okay?"

"So nice of you to ask, considering how I treated you, and Rob." Cindy heard what sounded like muffled sobbing on the other end. Was Emily all right? "Sorry," she said. "Needed to grab a tissue." After another pause, she continued. "Can you talk? I know it's late, but that's one of the old behaviors some AA members have. Late night phone calls."

Cindy hesitated. She had to get up early for a teachers' meeting. Still, Emily sounded needy. "Yes, go ahead."

Another sigh on the other end. "I know I was wrong to take Rob's kindness so seriously. I grabbed at it. But, what is it about him? That makes him that way?"

"Well," Cindy replied, "he is a man with a deep faith."

"Oh, a Christian?"

"Yes, didn't you know that?"

Cindy was fighting sleep. She really wanted this conversation to end. Then, she remembered the shooting star. Right over Emily's head. What was God showing her?

~

Rob picked Cindy up for the next AA meeting. Six pm. Was she able to deal with this again so soon? He wasn't sure, felt guilty. She had told him Emily called her. And, she had dealt with it. But, he still felt uncertain.

"Friday night meetings are kind of special," he said. "More like a party to celebrate another week of being sober. Cookies, sometimes cake, and flavored creamer." He pointed to a bakery box in the back seat. "Cake."

He glanced at Cindy, noticing a big smile on her radiant face. "You look happy."

"I am. A friend of mine got saved."

"Do I know her? I assume it's a her."

"Yes, you do. She was in the wedding." She looked over at him, still smiling. "Melanie."

"Wonderful! I didn't know she was in limbo about

her faith." Squeezing her hand quickly, he questioned Cindy. "What happened? Tell all, please."

"Private. Confidential. Secrets." She turned slightly in her seat. He wondered why she hesitated. Then, he understood. "Thanks in part to your mom."

"My mom brought Melanie to the Lord?"

"Partly, yes. She had a lot to do with it, taking her to Bible study and mostly listening to her. She's a special woman."

"Yep, sure is."

"I can't wait for her to be my mother-in-law." Cindy giggled. "Of course you have to do your part."

~

Cindy latched the door after Rob, disposed of the small amount of leftover Nachos, kicked off her high heels and changed barefoot into comfy, warm sweats. Today had been exciting and emotionally exhausting. After breakfast on Balboa Island at Wilma's Patio, they drove the short distance to Fashion Island shopping center and parked near Bloomingdale's. There was an upscale jewelry store almost right across from Bloomie's mall entrance that Rob wanted to check out. He had noticed unique designs in its windows when he had searched for an engagement ring for Cindy. Some of the designs were, in his opinion, a bit off the wall. But, were they timeless? Would they be dated in a few years?

Cindy pressed her nose against one display window of the store and squealed, so they went in. The middle-aged jeweler took the ring she had spied out of the window and laid it on a velvet-covered square on the counter. "Madam has excellent taste," he said in a slightly Aussie accent. She tried the opulent ring on and held out her hand to admire it. Then, she'd noticed the tiny sticker hanging on the platinum band and squealed again. She'd carefully removed the ring and said, "It is beautiful. But, not quite 'me.'" Gripping Rob's elbow tightly, she steered him out the door.

"What's the matter?" He looked puzzled. "I thought that ring was gorgeous, and," he exclaimed, "perfect on you."

"Rob, did you notice the price? Way, way too expensive." Her lips were set in a firm line.

"It was expensive. But, Cindy, my love, this is a once in a lifetime purchase. *For* a lifetime," he added. "Maybe on our fiftieth anniversary you can get another one," he quipped.

"Robinson Todd Lovejoy!" She had recently learned his middle name and loved to use it when badgering or teasing him. Why she hadn't known it before, she had no idea. Wasn't all that important, then. Now that it would soon be part of her name, her new name, it was important. "Even if you plan to replace it in fifty years, you will be eighty! And, retired. Maybe on a fixed income." She wiggled her nose at him and gripped his elbow harder.

"Well, then," he said nonchalantly, "you only get one. Forever." He tapped her nose with his index finger. "So, make a good choice." Cindy was sure he was joshing, and when he burst out laughing, she knew positively.

They traipsed through the mall to Traditional Jewelers. She hoped their prices were more traditional, too. They weren't, but they did have a much wider range of styles to choose from. Not only did they have Solitaire diamonds in all sizes (smaller was less expensive) and the square Princess cut diamonds, but they had pear-shaped, and even heart and star-shaped. She was tempted by the heart shapes, and especially the star shapes. Those she really loved – so unique. Then, she thought about how the points would probably catch on just about everything, especially sweaters and the adorable faces of three-year-olds. Not practical. At all. She was so confused and gripped Rob again by his elbow. They were about to leave when the owner of the store approached them.

"Don't I recognize you from Mariners Church?" he asked.

Impossible. There were probably around a thousand people at each service in two tiers of seating, and she usually sat up high to see the stage better. But, he was right. Of course he had a very good eye being a jeweler. She had heard he attended there. Then she remembered – he served on the board of elders. She had seen his name in the bulletin.

Cindy nodded, introduced herself and Rob who said in jest, "I attend there, too. But, I'm not as pretty." Mr. Owner laughed.

"I do recognize your last name. You own that floral shop in Corona del Mar?" he asked.

"My family does, mostly my brother. I'm a realtor."

"Oh, one of those. Just a rung above lawyers." The man laughed heartily, then redeemed himself. "Actually, I have seen your name next to well done real estate ads in the Saturday paper. Nice to meet you.

"May I show you a ring that I just designed? I can tell you are looking for something unique, but at the same time classic."

Rob shrugged, and Cindy nodded. She felt trapped. Was he talking about a ring the cost of a whole year's income? She couldn't do that to Rob, nor to their future. Marriage had so many expenses. She knew she was jumping ahead in her thinking, but worry took over. And, one thing she did want to spend money on was a beautiful wedding like Noelle had. She knew her dad was okay financially, but he was pushing retirement age and couldn't, or shouldn't, foot the bill for an extravagant wedding. If her mom had been alive, loving fancy events as she had, she would have pushed Dad. But, Cindy wanted to pay for a lot of the wedding herself. Fat chance on her preschool teacher's salary. She turned her attention back to Mr. Owner who was holding a lovely engagement ring in a piece of navy felt.

"Try it on," he said in a soft voice.

"I shouldn't." But, she did.

~

Now, with bare feet propped up on her glass coffee table, she wiggled into the soft pillows on the sofa and day-dreamed about the diamond on her empty finger. She imagined twisting it with some difficulty. What was unique about it, other than the gorgeous stone, was the square band. Cindy loved that. She reminisced about the several hours she and Rob had spent with the jeweler. It had been fun, and very educational. He'd explained about depth and carat and cut to them. Then, he made them an agreement. At first Cindy thought it was a deal, but it wasn't. It was merely a suggestion, one she and Rob delighted in.

Next Sunday at church, she and Rob would be signing up for the mission field!

CHAPTER FIFTEEN

She hadn't bothered to take off her sweats. She was comfy, tired and cold. The Newport Beach weather was a bit bitter tonight. Maybe it was the wind. She heard it whistling through the patio doors. She had thought many times about stuffing towels under them. If only she could remember before succumbing to sleep. She was stumbling into bed when the doorbell chimed. It was only eight-thirty, but she and Rob had had a fatiguing day, although very exciting. Her engagement ring would not be ready until February, the day before Valentine's Day. Something about the fit and getting the perfect diamond. She was okay with that, but it would be hard to wait. Who was ringing the bell? Mustering every bit of patience, she flipped the lock and opened the door. Probably shouldn't be so trusting.

Emily stood there holding a brown paper lunch bag.

"Ah, hi," Cindy managed to say. "But what are you doing here?"

Emily squirmed, then held out the bag. "Bringing you a present." The bag squirmed, too.

She placed it in Cindy's hands, and it squirmed again. "Should I open this? Is it going to bite me?" She had concerns. After all Emily had been in love with Rob. Maybe there was a snake in the bag.

"No, no. It's a special present. One I picked just for you. One I think you need, or at least should have." She smiled widely, and the bag wiggled more. "Open it."

A tiny gray paw poked out. Then a fluffy face with almond-shaped green eyes. Cindy put her nose to the open bag and it got licked.

~

Star. She had named the kitten Star, actually Shooting Star, but Star for short. Star was draped around her, her back legs across Cindy's neck and her front ones half tucked into the neckline of the gray sweat top. Her little pink wet nose nestled under Cindy's chin. How could she say no? She had always wanted a kitten, just never got around to it. But, from Emily?

After Cindy opened the paper bag and Star climbed onto her shoulder, Emily deposited a large white plastic trash bag inside, then left. Inside was a small plastic litter box, a bag of cat litter and scoop, and a large bag of kitty food. She had thought of it all. Almost.

Cindy scrounged up an old afghan and a cardboard box. That would do for a bed for Star. She couldn't believe she was doing this, and so unexpectedly. Somehow, she didn't mind, actually found the small creature with the gray and white face comforting. And so adorable.

She settled Star in her new bed and crawled under

the covers. Oops. Tiny needle-like claws dug into her shoulder. Then, a buzzing purr.

~

"I got a surprise last night," she held the phone away from her face. "From Emily." She was tempted to facetime him and show him Star, but she resisted. It would be fun to see the shock on his face in person. "See you soon. Dinner this time, not just Nachos."

Her doorbell rang in ten. Wow, that man was quick. Had he been parked just a block away? She picked up Star and put her in the big front pocket of her sweatshirt. She fit perfectly, even snuggled down for a nap.

"Hi. What's the surprise?" He looked puzzled, annoyed. "What did Emily give you? Something disgusting?"

"Kiss me, and I'll tell you." She stretched to reach his lips and snuggled close. "Or, maybe you can feel it." She was counting on Star doing her wiggling thing, and she wasn't disappointed.

"What is wrong with your stomach? I know you must be hungry, but I don't hear gurgling, just feel wiggling." Poor Rob. He looked so flustered.

"My tummy is fine. I just have something caught in my pocket. Can you fish it out?" She waited breathlessly while Rob put both hands in both side openings of the pocket. Then, he stopped. His eyes grew huge as he pulled Star out.

"Oh, my gosh! Is this what Emily gave you?" He held the tiny fur ball up to his face in one hand. Star almost disappeared in Rob's big paw. The cat mewed and started to nibble on his thumb. Cindy nodded and grinned. She hoped he wasn't allergic. She'd never thought to ask Lydia.

"You okay with this?"

"Actually, I am more than okay. Her name is Star, by the way."

"Wow. You must have fallen in love with her faster than you did with me."

"Well, she doesn't dance," Cindy teased. "But, if I lead, I suppose she could."

~

"Have you opened your mail today?" Rob held an envelope and drew a letter out.

"Not yet. Concern? Ring won't be ready when he said?" She was so focused on the ring. She had to get over that. It was only an item, a thing, and it didn't define their love.

"Nothing like that. It's a letter from Mariners about a choice of upcoming mission trips." He cocked his head. "You do remember agreeing to that, right?"

"Of course. I wasn't expecting it so soon." She fidgeted with the empty spot on the third finger of her left hand. "What's it say? Maybe I should check my own mail." She ran to the kitchen counter where today's mail was piled. Sorting through the envelopes she pulled out the one that had Mariners Church as the return address.

"Wow! Some of them are soon, like in four weeks."

"Yeh, too soon for us I think."

"Was that a question?"

"Sort of, but no," Rob said. "I think it might be more special to go after we are married, or at least officially engaged." He peered at the letter again. "Although it's not mandatory, they do like couples going to be married. Maybe they would make an exception for us?"

"Possibly. When would you want to go? And, to where?" There were several mission trips listed. Quite a few in Mexico. One in China. So far away, such a long one. One in Costa Rica. That was a good one.

"Rob, look at the last one ... in Costa Rica." She touched his hand hoping he, too, would pick up on that one. He grinned. She suddenly had the courage to continue. "We could get married there on the beach. Before, of course, the actual mission trip."

"A what do you call it, a destination wedding?" He looked back at the letter, and she was sure he looked puzzled.

CHAPTER SIXTEEN

Another letter. Both he and Cindy needed to have medical evaluations in order for Mariners Church to cover them with insurance for the mission. The mission wasn't scheduled until June – perfect month for a wedding. Especially on the beach. He was excited, but scared. Would they accept him going with his health issues? He made the doctor appointment and hoped.

Why had he never told her? It wasn't a life issue, but could be in ten years. Not fair to Cindy. He called Mom.

"You never told her? Never discussed it?" Mom sounded appalled. And angry. She seldom did, but this time she lit into him. "Robinson Todd," she said using his full given name like she did when he was three, "that was not fair to Cindy." Finally, she said in her most authoritative mom voice, "Do it now."

"We need to talk." That wasn't one of his best

intros. If he could have kicked himself he would have. Nerves.

When he arrived at her door he smelled the pungent odor of melting cheese. Last night had been special – the succulent chicken dripping in sauce. Yes, she was a super cook, and not just for Nachos. She claimed the recipe was from her Grandma, and it was a secret. But, tonight he only smelled her Nachos.

Rob settled himself on the red sofa and started to stuff his face. "Could we pray first, please?" she said.

"Sorry. Nervous."

"Why?"

"Gotta share. Should have a long time ago."

Cindy adjusted the throw pillows behind them and settled herself on the sofa deliberately at the other end from Rob. Placing her hands on her knees, "Well?"

"There is more about me than AA." He looked over to see her expression. Bewildered? Scared? This would not be easy.

"Cindy, do you know what MS is?"

"Not really. I know it's a disease, a debilitating one. So I've heard." She stopped and stared at him, like he had been caught in a time warp and was floating in putrid, decaying air. Finally, after a long, loud whoosh of a breath, she said, "You got it?"

~

Cindy wrung her hands, like Great Grammy Emma did when she was troubled, or praying. Somehow she came to her senses and shimmied over on the sofa to Rob. He didn't move a muscle, sat like a marble statue. She touched his leg. Not a quiver.

"Explain please."

He shifted a bit and placed his hand on hers. That

was a start.

"It's a progressive disease. Sometimes not very debilitating at all. So, there is hope. Do you remember the time at the shop I cut myself?"

She nodded. "Was that one of those times? Because …"

"Maybe, probably. Can't be sure. That is one of the mysteries of Multiple Sclerosis. It could just have been a fluke accident, or it could have been because I had minimal muscle control."

"How would we know either way?"

He realized she had said 'we,' and that gave him hope.

"We wouldn't for sure. Fortunately, I've had very few instances. Very few," he repeated firmly.

She gripped his hand. "There's no cure, is there?" Her eyes glistened as she looked him square in the face. "How did you discover you have it?"

"One day about two years ago Brad and Nick and I had been surfing at the Point. It was very early and bitter cold. I kept losing my balance walking back to the car, sure it was the mushy sand."

He closed his eyes and heard his friends' voices again.

"Stumble bum!"

"I thought you were a great dancer, Rob. And, you can't even navigate the beach."

"Give us the leash of your board, and we'll tow you."

Rob tilted his head back and closed his eyes. "They laughed and slapped my shoulders; guy stuff. I, too, thought it was just a quirk, that my muscles were reacting to the extreme cold."

Cindy nodded, "But?"

"My balance was fine the next few days. Then, about a week later, I stumbled getting into my car after an AA meeting. So embarrassing. The guys rushed to me, and Emily insisted I blow my breath in her face. The worst part was that they didn't trust me, thought I had been drinking."

Cindy squeezed his hand harder. "Go on. What happened next?

"I didn't start my car right away ... sat there for maybe ten minutes with the motor running. What scared me more than the balance issue was my left eye got blurry. Then, it went away and I drove home, slowly." He clung to Cindy's hand more tightly. She winced.

"Sorry. Sometimes I can't tell how strong, or how weak, I am. Comes and goes. But, the balance thing came back a few weeks later." He looked into her eyes. "I was scared. I thought maybe I had a brain tumor.

"With Mom's insistence, I went to the family doc who sent me to a neurologist who set me up for an MRI. I was so clueless, and so scared, I didn't even ask why, or what the docs were looking for."

Cindy nodded again. Her eyes were so wide they almost took over her face. "So?"

"Turns out they were looking for plaques on the spinal cord." He lowered his head. "They found them."

"And?" She kept asking one syllable questions. He assumed she was in a state of shock. After all, he was throwing all this at her the night before they would be officially engaged. What a jerk he was!

"I was in the early stages of MS." There, he'd finally explained it. Hadn't he?

Cindy rubbed the empty space on the ring finger of her left hand again. Tomorrow it would never be empty again ... if. Could she handle this situation with Rob? Forever? For a lifetime?

She reminded herself about the wedding vows, the through sickness and in health, and the until death do us part, and that no one but God knows our future. Holding her cellphone instead of a printed Bible, she pushed the prompts to Jerimiah 29:11. A much used scripture. One she had used when her mother died and when Doreen had her devastating accident. She loved that scripture. It was so confirming, filled her with hope. That's what she needed tonight – hope, for Rob and her.

She tried to push away the anger she had. She understood his reluctance to tell her, but when did he plan to do it? After they were engaged? Or, worse yet, married? He used the excuse of out of sight, or as he'd said, out of episodes, out of mind. He did explain that he hadn't had any symptoms for over a year, except the cut at the floral shop. And, he couldn't be sure it was a result of the disease; could simply have been a fluke. She thought back to the night he gave her the phony ring and how his knee popped twice. Could that have been a fluke, too? Now she wondered if he would stumble down the aisle on their wedding day or drop the ring. So many uncertainties, so many decisions. He was a marvelous dancer and had never stumbled, but held her firmly and led perfectly.

The mission! Oh, dear, what should they do about that? Her own doctor appointment for her well-check was in two days. When was Rob's?

She put her hand over her heart and wept. Tomorrow she would have to make a decision to accept the ring or call off the engagement.

CHAPTER SEVENTEEN

*T*oday was the day!

Rob had made a reservation for dinner at Mayur, one of her favorite restaurants. She loved Indian, and it had a private room usually reserved for groups. But, after explaining the reason, they agreed to reserve it for him.

He parked at Fashion Island and sat in his car and prayed. He needed to pray more. He did fly-by-night prayers in the shower every morning and quick ones when he crawled into bed. This was different. This was his future … with, or without, Cindy.

He felt a peace settle over him, struggled out of the car when his left leg wouldn't cooperate and managed to make his way stumbling to the jewelry store. Fortunately, he had parked in the lower lot so he was able to take the escalator that deposited him a short distance from the jewelry store. His legs seemed to cooperate during the brief walk.

The store was amazing. He hadn't paid much attention the day they were shopping for the ring, but now it blew his mind. It was circular, round, stood out from all the other stores in the mall. Huge, too. Had they made the right decision to purchase the ring at this opulent store? Maybe they should have gone to Los Angeles to the diamond area, or even to Costa Mesa or another neighboring city where prices were not so inflated.

He entered the huge glass doors and took a deep breath. Gotta be brave. And he had already made a commitment. Approaching the clerk behind the counter, he asked for Mr. Owner. He still didn't remember the man's name, but Owner should do the trick.

The clerk, an Indian man, bowed his head. "Owner passed away last week."

"What? How?"

"Suddenly. No reason, no warning. Just happened." The man bowed his head and asked why Rob was there.

~

Rob held the precious velvet box in his hand and stared at it. Finally, he put it in his pocket, got in his car and drove to Cindy's.

What were the magic words? The words to seal a lifetime of love, or erase them. Again, he sat in his car, this time outside of Cindy's condo. *Please, Lord, give me guidance and favor, and give me the courage to use Your guidance.*

His legs and arms fought him again, wobbly and very little control. Why of all times? He hadn't had an incident for almost a year.

Cindy answered the door with a smile on her face.

That was encouraging. Rob grinned.

She lifted her hands to cup them around Rob's cheeks. "I love you." Nuff said.

EPILOGUE

June

$\mathcal{L}$ydia Lovejoy fussed with her pale blue MOG gown. She was again the Mother of the Groom, and she was thrilled. She looked out the window of the small rented cottage on sticks the locals called a bungalow. Logan came up behind her and kissed her on the neck.

"Don't spoil my makeup!" She elbowed him, then turned around for a full kiss. "This is exquisite; this setting; a perfect place to have a perfect wedding."

Logan hugged her. "You think Braydon will be jealous? Not getting married here in Costa Rica on the beach?"

"Not at all. He and Noelle married in the perfect place for them at Sherman Gardens. This is perfect for Rob and Cindy." She paused to breathe in the fresh salt air of the ocean only a hundred yards away. "Their mission is perfect, too. With God's will they can plant a small church. Cindy can start a preschool; Christian, of course. Rob can start support groups for MS and join the local AA meetings."

Logan nodded. "What a blessing Rob found this place through AA friends. That Brian guy who manages the bungalow rentals is super. It's even better that he lives here full time. And," he added, "his boys are adorable."

"Cute names, too. Fletch and Hux. Their mother must have chosen them, you think?"

"I asked him about their names. He said he'd had naming rights."

They watched as a group of musicians collected on the beach. One of them was the Brian guy who had a guitar slung over his shoulder. Each carried a folding chair, set it up in a semi-circle making sure the feet were anchored in the sand. A little dog raced behind them. Brian settled it down with a gesture of his hand. Must be his dog. His little boys followed the dog that had a bow tie around its neck. The boys were dressed in surfer shorts with blue Hawaiian shirts.

Lydia remembered the boys were to act as ring bearers. She knew Cindy would have loved to have some of her students perform that part, but even though airfare was reduced, it was too much to ask. However, the kids would have gotten free surfing lessons from Brian.

The music started to play, and Lydia and Logan walked out to the wide porch to wait their turn. Since Cindy's mother was deceased, Lydia would be the first woman to be escorted down the sandy aisle. She thanked God that Cindy's dad who was compromised with arthritis and a fixed income was able to attend. He would walk her down the aisle on the white fabric the wedding coordinators had placed. She prayed he wouldn't trip.

She also prayed Robinson would not have an episode. MS can be so random, and often reveals its ugly head when one is nervous.

She saw a large black car pull up on the narrow dirt road between the bungalows and the beach. Four people piled out. Rob, Noelle and Braydon, and someone who looked like a possible preacher who was dressed in board shorts, flip flop sandals and a white button down shirt with a black bow tie at the neck. It did look as if he was carrying a book. Hopefully, a Bible. He held it to his chest and made his way to the end of the white fabric aisle where a lovely arch was set up and covered with vines and roses. A makeshift altar of wood and palm fronds rested beneath the arch. It was adorned with a long white crocheted scarf that Cindy had told her belonged to her mother and had been made by her grandmother. It was a way to honor both of them and have them be part of the nuptials. Resting in the center was a cross made completely of sea shells that young Taylor had designed and made with help from her siblings.

The preacher gestured to the musicians. They nodded and started to play their version of something classical. Chopin? It was a little funky, a bit off tune, but it worked to provide background music while guests were taking their seats.

Braydon stepped forward in navy board shorts and escorted his mother down the makeshift aisle with Logan following. Lydia was so proud of her sons she almost burst. She grinned over at Kerstin Day, Noelle's mother, who was seated opposite her with Darrell. She was certain Kerstin's eyes were moist like hers.

She shouldn't break protocol and turn around, but she did. She noticed Dana emerged from Bungalow 5, next to theirs. She had her four children in tow and guided them forward to take their part in the ceremony. Shady was to join Fletch and Hux to be a ring bearer. Lydia wondered how many rings there could possibly be, but each boy held a small pillow in front of him. She was sure the rings tied on them were totally fake. Just a fun part of the ceremony. Shyla would be a flower girl tossing petals profusely on the white cloth runner.

Lydia was so glad the wedding coordinator was Jill who had helped Kerstin plan Noelle's and Braydon's wedding. The woman was a fount of information, and so accommodating. If not for her careful planning, the flowers for the bouquets and the loose rose pedals for the flower girl to fling (which she did dramatically) would not have arrived to this semi-remote destination. They certainly couldn't have been shipped to this third world country, because they would never have arrived at the wedding and would be gracing the arms of the postal workers' women. Instead, they were carried in several guests' baggage wrapped in Cellophane and foil, little plastic water tubes on each stem to keep them moist. In order for them to pass security inspection a tag was tacked on to each bloom and the plastic box of petals that said Made in U.S.A. as Brian had advised them to do.

Lydia and Jill had held their breaths while going through Customs with the Days and other guests, but they made it. Perhaps it was the large U.S. bill of currency Logan slipped into a Customs officers paw. When Lydia's enormous suitcase slid topsy-turvy off the whooshing conveyer belt with only one latch open, she let out a huge sigh of relief.

She brought her mind to the moment at hand, the wedding, and thought about all the details and planning that had gone into it.

She had tried to convince the couple to have a beach wedding in Newport, or anywhere in California. But, they were insistent. Costa Rica was where God had led them to plant a church and establish therapy groups for MS sufferers. Were they qualified for either? She turned her thoughts back to the numerous attendants. Such a special group.

Dana's eldest child Taylor would be a junior bridesmaid. She was dressed in her favorite color of blue and held her head high, strands of her long hair escaping the curls and framing her face. Robert the stylist they'd brought from California had spent hours producing exceptional hairstyles for all the women and girls. This was eleven-year-old Taylor's moment, and Lydia was sure it would be forever in her memory.

Lydia had wondered about the keyboard set up on a small low table in front of the diverse collection of musicians. Perhaps someone hadn't shown up. Being partially turned around, she almost missed the keyboard player. Eight-year-old Teagan quietly settled herself sliding onto the mock piano bench, adjusted her blue skirt and grinned shyly. Lydia knew from talking with Dana that Teagan hated to be the center of attention. But, somehow Dana had talked her into it. Maybe it was partly Ms. Lorrie and the fact her ten-year-old granddaughter Swae had played the piano at a recent wedding. Something had given Teagan courage.

She softly played the Ode to Joy Beethoven piece

her tutor Mrs. Prince had practiced with her for weeks. They had also practiced the Wedding March daily until Teagan's fingers were numb.

After all the guests and Lydia and Logan were seated, the pastor nodded to her. Teagan's slender fingers hovered over the keyboard to play Someday My Prince Will Come just as Cindy's prince charming took his place in front of the officiant. Lydia was not sure where he'd come from. Obviously out of that long limo, then probably hiding behind the row of upright surf boards lined up at the side. So, that was the purpose of them! Braydon followed him as his Best Man. Two other men followed. One had long blond hair tied in a ponytail, the other's dark hair was short cropped, almost shaved. Lydia recognized them as his surfer buddies, Nick and Brad.

If she hadn't been so curious, well nosy actually, she might have missed Arthur Akers walking from another bungalow and pausing next to his daughter. Lydia wasn't sure, but even from her distance, as they turned to each other, she thought both of them had moist eyes. She was delighted that Arthur was not wearing board shorts, though. His navy linen pants and jacket and his graying temples made him look very distinguished.

She could see that Cindy wore a diaphanous white gown that seemed to float delicately around her, like air. Robinson and his attendants were all clad in board shorts and topped with tuxedo jackets and vests, even with four in hand ties! She had expected Hawaiian print shirts.

Rob stood rigidly in front of the pastor. The music pumped up, and the children led the procession. The boys started to race, as boys do, down the aisle as a cute canine joined them. Lucy, the French Bulldog raced with a ribbon hanging out of her mouth. She sat obediently at the feet of Fletch and wiggled proud. Lydia could see something metallic hung from the ribbon in the dog's mouth. Surely, it wasn't one of the real rings. Little Shy skipped and gleefully threw handfuls of petals randomly, and obviously with abandon, some landing on guests laps or hitting them in faces.

After the giggling died down, Taylor stepped forward. She stepped slowly, smiled and held her beautiful rose nosegay in front of her perfectly. She was followed by five other women, all Candy Canes. For this wedding they were dressed in sea green blue, probably Cindy's choice to give emphasis to the climate and the beach venue. Their bouquets of buttery white roses whose petals were tinged with blue matched Taylor's. Lydia was thrilled with the gorgeous bouquets. She knew Braydon had worked all morning with Jill's assistant to design them. Later, in early afternoon, Lydia and Braydon created Cindy's bridal bouquet, one Lydia had specifically designed for her, as she had Noelle's over a year ago. It was her gift to Cindy. She was so glad she had taken that floral design course from Marg in Scottsdale several years ago. Not only was Marg Rodger a dear, but she was an award-winning floral designer who had shared her brilliant creations and how to compose them with Lydia. It was because of Marg that Lydia had the gumption to open Love In Bloom in Corona del Mar. Now, she was seeing her own creation being held by her future daughter-in-law.

It was larger than she'd originally planned, but the thirteen roses formed a perfect heart. Lydia had wanted it to be both special and make a statement. Tiny white fluffy wax flowers bordered the roses like a delicate frame; tissue white Seafoam Statice and white Ginestra flowed from the bouquet dramatized with slender leaves of lily grass, and three white Cymbidium Orchids that she had grown herself nestled at the heart tip of the pure white rose blossoms. The trailing blooms added an elegant softening effect, and the orchids were to symbolize the Trinity. Lydia was thrilled with the resulting bouquet. But, she reminded herself, this wedding wasn't about her.

Melanie was the first bridesmaid followed by Candy, Natalie, and Connie. Tall, elegant Doreen was last, the only one in a long skirt to hide her shoe lift. The musicians paused while the women arranged themselves in a charming group. Lydia thought they were all so poised, such lovely young women. She was grateful to have them in her life. She felt a bit like a house mother, and she knew Kerstin Day felt the same.

Soft music announced the Matron of Honor, her beautiful daughter-in-law Noelle. Noelle's gown was a deeper blue with some lace detail on the skirt and bodice. All were strapless, except young Taylor's and her sisters'. Little cap sleeves were perfect on them. Connie had designed all of them except the little girls' that she had taken to her favorite dressmaker Sandy who copied the bridesmaid dresses in miniature and added the cute little sleeves.

Lydia noticed all the girls and women wore fancy thong sandals with rhinestones and pearls on them. Most appropriate for a surfside wedding. Robinson and

Cindy had given each girl and woman a special necklace, a delicate ring encased in rhinestones with a small heart in the middle. What a special token to save for their own weddings someday. The little girls' and Noelle's and Connie's and Natalie's and Melanie's were sterling silver, but Doreen's and Candy's were gold. Lydia learned later that Cindy had chosen the necklace colors after observing the jewelry each girl wore. Cindy had also given her the same necklace in gold to match her wedding band, but it had tiny pearls alternating on the delicate chain, and she was sure the stones in hers were diamond chips and the metal 18K. She fingered it, and her heart swelled with joy.

She was so glad she had played the mother card with Robinson insisting he tell Cindy about the MS diagnosis. Going into a marriage with secrets was no way to begin one.

Noelle had reached the end of the aisle with delicate steps. She shifted her bouquet to her left arm in readiness to take Cindy's when she arrived. All the attendants turned to face the back of the aisle when Teagan struck a chord and led the little musician group in the traditional Wedding March. Everyone stood up and faced the bride who practically floated on her father's arm.

"Who gives this woman in holy matrimony?" The pastor's strong voice rang out.

"I do," Arthur Akers said. "With blessings," he added. As he turned to sit in the first row next to the Days, a chorus of voices resounded, "We do, too!" There was a beaming smile on every Candy Cane face, and the pastor almost dropped his Bible.

~

Because of the unpredictable sea breeze, there were no candles, so she and Arthur Akers wouldn't be lighting a unity candle. Instead, she, Logan and Cindy's dad would clasp hands in front of the cross while the preacher (hopefully, he was one) said a blessing over the families by reading from Psalm 112.
Praise the LORD.
>Blessed are those who fear the LORD,
who find great delight in his commands.
² Their children will be mighty in the land;
the generation of the upright will be blessed.
³ Wealth and riches are in their houses,
and their righteousness endures forever.

~

The three parents returned to their seats and dabbed their eyes. Lydia guessed he probably was a real, ordained pastor since he had chosen such a lovely scripture to bless them with. She hoped.

She was smoothing her dress – why was she fussing with it again? – when the pastor's deep voice rang out.

"Ladies and gentlemen, this is usually the time when I would expound on the importance of Holy Matrimony." He smiled broadly. "But, having met with the bride and groom and having learned of their life plans," his eyes scanned the guests, "and why they chose to marry in this glorious setting, I have decided the following passage from Isaiah 58 eleven and twelve says it perfectly, as God's Word always does." He cleared his throat and raised a hand over Rob and Cindy as he read the ancient words.

"I'll give you a full life in the emptiest of places—firm muscles, strong bones. You'll be like a well-watered garden, a gurgling spring that never runs dry. You'll use the old rubble of past lives to build anew, rebuild the foundations from out of your past. You'll be known as those who can fix anything, restore old ruins, rebuild and renovate, make the community livable again."

Lydia was blown away. This scripture was perfect for Rob and Cindy, for the reason they were here, for their mission in Costa Rica, and especially for their marriage commitment. She brought her hands together between her breasts, the breasts she had nurtured Rob with thirty years ago.

~

"… for better or for worse, in sickness and in health, till death do us part."

That part of the vows frightened Lydia. But when she saw Cindy turn toward Rob with a beaming face, she relaxed. In a few minutes she would have another amazing daughter-in-law.

Noelle slid a ring off her right hand to pass to the clergyman to bless. When Braydon fished in his pocket for Cindy's ring she was thankful it wasn't secured on one of the many ring bearers' satin pillows, and especially not on Lucy the dog's ribbon. Braydon passed it to the minister who blessed it and placed it carefully in Rob's palm. Rob stared at it for a long moment. Was he having an incident? Finally, Rob looked at Cindy, his eyes glassy with tears. His whisper was just loud enough for those in the front rows to hear. "I still can't believe this is happening. Thank you, Lord, for this wonderful gift, this woman You have given me." Then he placed the ring on her finger.

Lydia found herself being escorted back up the

aisle by Nick. She had done this before, played this part before. She felt a little confused when Logan gave her a gentle push. She was following Cindy's dad, Arthur. He was not being escorted, but Brad had gestured he should start walking and walked behind him. He looked so alone, and in her usual style, she prayed for him.

She thought about the fact both her boys had married only children. A coincidence, or God's plan? Noelle at least had a mother, a wonderful one who had become Lydia's dear friend. But, Cindy only had her. Could she fill that role?

She found herself and Logan piling into a limousine. They were deposited with aplomb at a huge Marriott Hotel. Knowing Arthur Akers couldn't afford this extravagance, she and Logan had paid for a reception with the hotel's exceptional fare, and best of all, dancing. She prayed Cindy would never know, never feel obliged. It was the Lovejoy's treat for her and their son.

Rushing to the ladies' room, Lydia couldn't help but overhear spattered conversations.

"Gorgeous wedding!'

"Special on the beach."

"The groomsmen were hunks." A giggle or two followed that one.

Then, "How do you suppose Rob and Cindy afforded to pay for this extravagance?"

"Not our business. Just enjoy the moment." She liked that one, wished she knew who said it.

Another one. "Let's just go have fun. Wonder if Emily is here?"

Who was Emily? Lydia didn't know that name. Should she worry?

She joined the crowd in the ballroom, found her place with Logan and Arthur at the special table reserved for them. She noticed a small table, was it called a Sweetheart Table? Close to the band? Suddenly, a band blast, a pause, and a tapping of drums and loud guitar stringing.

"Ladies and gentlemen, I present the bride and groom. Mr. and Mrs. Robinson Todd Lovejoy!"

~

Cindy's eyes lit up like sparklers. Rob was so proud of her and so much in love. He took her hand and led her into the ballroom decorated with globe lights hanging below drapes of tulle billowing from the ceiling and smelling of roses. He kissed her and led her to the tiny table in front of the band. Everyone clapped and some even cheered.

"Rob?" Her cheeks were rosy and her eyes brimmed. With joy, he hoped. "How did this happen? It is so extravagant."

He shrugged. "Just did." That was all he'd explain. Later, when they were in Bungalow Three after two nights at the Marriott, he would ... maybe ... share with her. After she had donned the elegant nightgown Connie had whispered to him about, the one she had designed. Or, maybe a lot later, after she, or he, had removed it. Maybe never.

He lifted her hand and pulled her up. "Rob, it's not yet time for the first dance."

He nodded to the small band. They took the cue playing "Get the party started."

Did it really matter that the first dance was protocol?

"Cindy," he said as he nuzzled her ear. "Let's

dance."

THE END

Keep reading for a yummy recipe and the first chapter of book 3, Candy's Wild Ride

CHAPTER ONE

"*I* am Cinderella, with no fairytale prince."

Natalie whispered to herself and tossed her ponytail over her shoulder before she started wiping down the free weights. Was this what her life had come to? Cleaning stuff? She was grateful for her small gym and the local residents who had joined it and used it almost daily. Some of them said they were uncomfortable in the huge workout areas of the chain gyms. They liked the more intimate surroundings, chatting with neighbors who they actually knew, not someone in another zip code.

But, she didn't have enough members to pay the bills.

It was six o'clock and she was about to close up for the day when Bill walked in.

"Am I too late?"

He was a new member she'd only seen once or twice. But, he caught her attention this evening, maybe with his question. He had a full head of graying hair, a firm face with few wrinkles and a wide smile. What seemed like a genuine one, not a come on. He was very attractive for an older man, and her heart skipped a beat.

She guessed him to be fifty plus. Maybe thirty years older than her. Did that matter? Melanie's stepfather Bruce was in his fifties. But, Melanie hated him. Still, Bill had always been a gentleman the few times she had seen him here. Being a black belt in karate, she felt comfortable with any male coming late to her gym.

She had been inspired to start the gym right after high school when her swim coach mentor Coach Douglas encouraged her. He had been supportive of all the Candy Cane swim team members' dreams for the future, but because she wanted to encourage physical health, he offered to make a small investment in Natalie's gym. He died before he could make it legal, nor support any of the other Candy Canes' endeavors. The other girls had pursued other dreams. Noelle had married Braydon who owned Love In Joy Floral Shop in Corona del Mar, and she was teaching English at Vista del Mar High School. Melanie was working at New Hope Preschool in aftercare, but would soon be promoted to teacher. Cindy had married her dream man on the beach in Costa Rica. She and Rob were missionaries planning to plant a church there and establish groups to support Multiple Sclerosis suffers. All important stuff. Connie was a fashion designer, and Doreen was one of her models. Candy had gotten married young, divorced and never pursued a career. Of all of them she was hands down the most beautiful.

What did Natalie have? She just ran a small gym. One that only attracted locals, mostly because they knew her. Her client base was small.

Dialing her phone, she called Candy, the encourager. After all, what were Candy Canes for? They were such a tight knit group, and they always prayed for each other.

~

"Me, too," Candy said when Natalie told her she was down in the dumps. "Do you think it's our age?"

Natalie laughed at that. "Maybe. But, hey, we ain't *that* old, girl."

"How about single?" Candy retorted.

"Candy," Natalie almost yelled. "We are only twenty-six. Not over the hill yet. In our prime. Still able to reproduce." Why had she said that? Was she desperate to have children, a family?

~

Bill came in the following morning. Early this time, real early. She said a simple "Hi" and went back to stacking free weights in their proper places. So frustrating that people used them and left them near machines or on the floor. Why hadn't she noticed them last night when she was wiping down? Maybe Bill coming in late distracted her.

This morning he waved and jumped on the treadmill, amping it up to high intensity. She could tell by the loud whirring sound. Last night he wore workout shorts and a short-sleeved tee. Today he wore long workout pants with a stripe down the legs and a tee shirt that hugged his biceps. Not bad ones for an older guy.

What was she thinking? Was she so desperate she was drawn to a man more than twice her age? He seemed a very nice man, a man who was almost handsome and was pleasant and courteous. But, what did she know about him? Maybe he was married, although no ring. But, many men of his era didn't wear rings. Wearing wedding bands was more of a millennial thing. Forget it, Natalie. Find another dream.

Several more clients came in. Kerstin Day, Noelle's mother, with a neighbor of hers. Natalie really should make more of an effort to memorize each client's name. When the gym started to fill up, she went to her office to do paper work. Bryce, her one personal trainer, clocked in and started to work with Kerstin. He was a blessing. All the clients loved him. If more clients wanted personal training at the same time, she would jump in. Unless she was giving a class.

She was paying her rent bill online and wondering how she would get through the next month. She looked at the sparse stack of checks on her desk. Some clients were late again. She felt uncomfortable reminding them, but business was business. She couldn't survive without their monthly payments. When she mentioned it the women would reach into their purses and pull out a check book. But, men almost always had to go to their cars and usually came back with cash. Then she had to write receipts. What was it with men and cash?

She flipped the lid closed on her laptop just as she heard a tapping. Bill was smiling at her through the speckled glass insert of the door. He was so tall the top of his head was cut off from view. What could he want? He had already paid his bill as he did punctually on the first of every month. Maybe he wanted to report a damaged machine. She opened the door and smiled.

"May I come in? Want to chat with you about something, an idea."

She gestured to the straight back wood chair and returned to her own chair behind the desk. He perched on the edge of his mopping his forehead with a small white towel.

"What's up, Bill?" She hoped she didn't sound too

confrontational, but she was due to start a Zumba class in ten minutes.

"Bad time? Sorry. I know you have a schedule to keep." he said. "This won't take long, but if it's something you are interested in discussing more, we could do so over coffee later."

Natalie nodded and squeezed her hands together on her desk.

"I've been thinking." He flung the towel around his neck.

She started to fidget. Would he ever get to the point? Then his face broke into that warm smile she liked so much, and the words from his mouth stunned her. Was he serious?

Bonnie Engstrom

Cindy's Nachos Recipe
Serves 4-6

Ingredients: (Do not let the list intimidate you. You probably have it all.)

* 1/2 to whole bag nacho chips (If your market has the latest $2 Only ones, they are the crispest and thinnest, the best)
* 1/2 jar of Medium salsa con queso warmed in microwave on low to soften
* 4 oz. shredded Sharp Cheddar cheese
* Crumbled blue cheese (a small amount crumbled in your fingers, lick off what is left!)
* A 4 oz. jar of sliced black olives (drain well, sprinkle liberally)
* 1 or 2 Roma tomatoes chopped (or whatever tomato you have)
* 1/2 to whole avocado chopped up (be sure it is firm, not mushy)
* Good salsa (sometimes generic is better, make sure it's mild; fresh is always better)
* Green onion chopped, but only if you have it.
* Sour cream to glob on top after chips are out of the micro

Assemble: (Just go for it.)

* Spray large micro safe platter with a bit of Pam.
* Start to assemble; chips first, top with other ingredients in order.
* The Key to unique is the Blue Cheese!
* The key to wonderful is liberally sprinkling all other ingredients over all.

* Microwave with caution. Start with 2 minutes on low, then go to 1 minute on high. You can always micro more, not less.

If you have it, sprinkle with fresh chopped cilantro for color and a little zest.

Everyone makes Nachos, but the secret ingredient in these is the blue cheese.

Have lots of napkins handy, and enjoy!

I hope by now you have read **Cindy's Perfect Dance** and suffered with her decisions. Her faith and her love came through.

Candy, too, is having a rough ride, both figuratively and literally. To be part of her dilemma and guide her be sure to read **<u>Candy's Wild Ride</u>** the next in the **Candy Cane Promise Sisters** series. Hop on and be sure to wear your helmet!

Next is the story about how Jake The Dawg helped Connie make the biggest decision of her life. After all, does a couture designer and a banker belong together? Jake thinks so.

Click **<u>here</u>** to order **Connie's Silver Shoes**, Book Four in the series. It's my favorite.

To order the entire **Candy Cane** series check **<u>here</u>**.

ABOUT THE AUTHOR

Bonnie Engstrom and her psychologist husband, Dave, live in Arizona near four of their six grandchildren. The other two live in Costa Rica where they surf. The couple share their Arizona home with Sam and Lola, their two rescued mutts in charge of the household.

She used to bake dozens of Christmas cookies in November and freeze them so she would have a lot to pass out to neighbors. Now ... well, that was a long time ago. Instead of cookies for Christmas, she writes. Her Candy Cane stories set in Newport Beach, California, where her family was raised and where they have many fond memories, are perfect for gift giving. Or, for just cuddling up by the fire for an inspiring romance read.

She hopes you enjoy Her Valentine Promise and also gift it to a special female in your life. Don't forget to leave an honest review on Amazon.

Milton Keynes UK
Ingram Content Group UK Ltd.
UKHW010659160724
445389UK00013B/690